Also by Joyce Mandeville

A TWIST OF LIGHT

CAREFUL
MISTAKES

Joyce Mandeville

WARNER BOOKS

A *Warner* Book

First published in Great Britain in 1996
by Little, Brown and Company
This edition published in 1997
by Warner Books

A CIP catalogue record for this book
is available from the British Library.

ISBN 0 7515 1671 6

Printed and bound in Great Britain
by Clays Ltd, St Ives plc

Warner Books
A Division of
Little, Brown and Company (UK)
Brettenham House
Lancaster Place
London WC2E 7EN

**To my mother, Doris Challstrom,
a woman of amazing grace**

ACKNOWLEDGEMENTS

Special thanks to my agent, Serafina Clarke, for leading me through the process of publication with patience and good humour. For endless re-readings and red pencil marks I owe a debt of gratitude to my dear friends, Heather O'Brophy and Peta Linley-Munro. My daughter Amy and her many insights were invaluable and I thank her with all my heart. Certainly not least, I thank my husband and son for their acceptance of my living in my own world for hours at a time.

CAREFUL
MISTAKES

CHAPTER ONE

Until you've sat a death watch you can't understand how exciting a trip to the airport can be. I pulled out of the palace gate feeling fifty pounds lighter and ten years younger.

When someone has been dying for weeks, death fills a chair at the table, uses its own towels, and sets all the clocks. Death decides if anyone in the house will sleep, what they will eat, what they will read, and death decides if anyone will have clean underwear.

My father, the Bishop, had announced to me, and to everyone else, that the cancer which had attacked his system three years before was now beyond treatment. He used the last of his strength writing letters, making lists, and receiving uncounted visitors. He had remained cheerful, alert, even funny until three weeks before when he had lapsed into a coma.

I left the palace knowing he was watched over. His nurse, Laura, was a sweet-faced, hardheaded, lapsed Roman Catholic from Belfast. She often told my father if she ever became a believer again she would become an Episcopalian because of him. She told him she liked the idea of a priest and bishop having children he could admit to. In addition to Laura, I could count on at least two to three members of various parishes in the tiny private chapel praying for his soul and ready reception into that Anglican paradise he seemed so sure of.

Chloe, my daughter, was coming home for spring break. She wasn't coming home for the death watch, but I was glad the two coincided. Although she loved her grandfather, at eighteen her world had pushed far beyond the Bishop's palace. It seemed right that she would see him die. I wanted her to see the normalcy of a good man having a good end.

Chloe had never been comfortable discussing death or its rituals. Unlike her peers, she had an aversion to horror films and books. When she was little she was always something pretty for Halloween. She never went into the haunted house ride at the fair. She didn't play with a ouija board at summercamp, and she always left the campfire when the ghost stories started. She would never visit the family crypt on her father's birthday, though I never knew why I felt I had to be there anyway.

Rick would be proud of Chloe now. He was so smitten with her, with being a husband, being a father. Sometimes I've been almost jealous of Rick. In Chloe's eyes he was perfect. The father who, had he lived, would have shielded her from every scraped knee, every punishment, every broken heart. The father who would have let her soar, unbound by a Bishop's home and a widow's fears.

The connection between mother and child never ends. We study the moods and phases of our children from the first flutter in the womb. We study the eyebrow, the shoulder, the toss of a hand, and we know.

She is tall, so I saw the top of her head first. Tawny curls, Rick's hair grown long, framing a Maxfield Parrish face. The long-limbed elegant nymph of sentimental posters geared out in khaki and wool. The eyes, green and round with fear, gave her away. Chloe wore the fear like a scarf wrapped around her face. She walked toward me, and I tried to decide if I should pretend her fear was for her grandfather.

Pushing past slower travelers, she walked into my arms, and I felt her go limp against me. 'Honey, what's wrong?' I needed to know. There seemed no point in pretending.

'I just want to go home. I've only got carry-on luggage. Just take me home.' Her voice was pitched higher than usual and sounded shrill to my ears.

'Sure. Let me take one of those.' I took a bag off her shoulder and elbowed my way through the airport crowd toward the door. It slid open with an electronic clunk. I glanced back to make sure she was behind me and smiled at her. The corner of her mouth twitched in response, then she looked away.

We walked into the bright sunlight and I slid the sunglasses from the top of my head to my face. 'How was your flight?' I started fishing. Eighteen years of mothering the girl had taught me how to draw information from her.

'It was a flight. Same oh, same oh. I'm sorry, Mom, I forgot to ask about Grandpa. What's going on?' She scanned the parking lot, looking for the car, I assumed.

'The car is over there. We can talk in the car.' I walked quickly, feeling her behind me. I needed to gather my wits. After a separation, she always talked a mile a minute, was always excited to be home. Even with the old man dying, the prospect of home should have charged her, lightened her step.

I opened the trunk of the car and helped her toss her bags in, then unlocked both sides from my door and slid into the driver's seat. I put on my seatbelt and turned toward Chloe. I touched the roll of hair at the back of my neck and glanced in the rearview mirror. An old habit that reminds me who I am.

'You asked about your grandfather. He is still in a coma. I'm told we are no longer looking at days but hours. You haven't had any calls. Now, I need to know right now, what's wrong?' I hated the sound of my voice, probing at her, wheedling for information.

'You've got to know I didn't want this to happen. I never wanted to hurt you. I don't know what to do.' She grabbed her arms and leaned forward, sobbing.

I rolled down my window to let fresh air into the car. I reached over and kissed her cheek, fighting an urge to scream. 'How far along are you?'

She didn't look at me, but she stopped crying with a start. She drew a few, ragged breaths. 'I'm two weeks late. I know I'm pregnant. I took three different tests. I started throwing up yesterday. I got sick twice on the flight. How could I have been so stupid?'

'Jesus Christ, Chloe. You were supposed to be the one bright spot in my day. How did this happen? How many times have I given you the responsible sexuality speech?' Dear God, why now? My father is dying and my eighteen-year-old is pregnant. Give me strength. I reached over and patted her hand. 'Listen, I'm sorry I said that. We need to get back. I love you, and you haven't hurt or disappointed me.' I love you and I could wring your neck right now. When this is over, I'm going to lock you in the attic until menopause – yours, not mine.

I pulled Dad's old Jag out of the parking lot, grateful to have something to do with my hands, someplace to focus my gaze. I wasn't shocked. Men, women, sex, and babies. It was the way things were supposed to be. Just not for Chloe, not yet.

Chloe was an exceptional girl. Brilliant – a college senior at eighteen, tawny and sleek, charming, kind. An only child raised by a widowed mother and scholarly grandparents, she was wise beyond her years. She was scheduled to begin work on her Master's in Anthropology in July, to spend the next twelve months in Oaxaxo, Mexico. This wasn't supposed to happen to Chloe. This had happened to Chloe.

'Chloe, I've always put you first, and I know you need me to do that now, but I just can't. We've got to put your grandfather first right now. We don't expect him to last the next twenty-four hours. When he's gone . . .' I felt myself beginning to choke. 'When he's gone, I'll help you look at everything. We will find help for you. Do you understand?' Death was my new speciality. I fancied that I had a gift for it. I adjusted my driving gloves as I steered the car toward home. I had begun taking care of my skin as I watched my father's deteriorate, to mottle and bruise.

'I understand. My timing is extremely shitty. I know what you've been going through. I'm sorry.' She began to cry again. For herself, for me, or for him?

'Don't worry about me. Dad has made this pretty easy for me. I've got good help, and he has been an amazingly good patient. It's been very bittersweet actually.' It has been harder than hell. I haven't slept for more than three hours at a time for two months. I'm tired and sad and my daughter is pregnant. On the plus side, my hands look pretty good.

We drove in silence through the spring countryside. Patches of snow clumped in shady spots. A few crocuses and snowdrops had forced themselves through the muddy ground. The trees were still bare but in a few days the buds would begin. Within a month the hills would be green under a canopy of pale, young leaves.

'Will he know I'm there?' Good girl. She was shifting gears, pulling out, if even for a few minutes.

'The hearing is supposedly the last thing to go. Laura and I tell everyone to speak to him as though he can hear. Maybe something gets through. I like to think so. I'm only letting three or four of his oldest friends in. Laura has been incredible. She takes care of bathing, linens, that sort of thing. Technically, she works the day shift, but she often stays until about eight in the evening. I'm on my own at night, but there is really nothing left to do then but give him injections.' No longer the daughter, I am now the mid-wife of death.

She looked out the window, seeming to ignore what I'd just said. 'Sometimes I really miss Connecticut.' Chloe was at U C Berkeley near San Francisco. Three years before, she'd wanted to be as far away as possible from New England.

'You can always come back for grad school. They've got Anthropology here too.'

Neither of us said anything. Because of a quickly divid-ing clump of cells, her future had changed forever. Birth or abortion. Abortion or birth. Problems are temporary. Solutions are permanent.

She sat up straighter as I turned down the road toward the palace. She reminded me of one of the dogs. Glad to go, but thrilled to be back.

Chloe and I moved into the palace when she was eigh-teen months old. She remembers nothing of her father's house. My father had come to tell me that Rick had been killed on the thruway. He filled a diaper bag, picked up Chloe, and put us in the back seat of his car.

My mother was in Manhattan when she heard the news. We arrived at the palace at the same time, and she led me to my old room. Chloe's nursery was waiting for her, since she was a frequent visitor. I'm not sure when or even if I decided to stay. I sold Rick's house, redecorated my room, and fell into the rhythms of my girlhood home. My parents grew old, and the house seemed more and more my own. When Mother died she left it to me.

Old timers refer to the palace as the Wolden Place. My mother was a Wolden. The Woldens have been here since before the Revolution. A comfortable, respectable family. My mother used to say that the Woldens had enough money, but not too much. We didn't have enough money to automatically be crazy or beautiful. My mother was neither beautiful nor crazy. While at Radcliffe she had fallen in love with a handsome theological student from Kansas. He had a scholarship, and she had a trust fund. She was a debutante and he was ambitious. It proved to be an excellent match.

When my father was ordained, it was a simple matter for my grandfather, a well-connected, well-respected Episcopalian, to have my father appointed to the cathedral ten miles away from the Wolden Place. Fifteen years later my father was elected Bishop, and the Wolden Place became the Bishop's palace.

The palace is actually one of the few bishop's palaces that even vaguely lives up to the name. The average bishop lives on a fairly modest income and housing allowance. My father was fortunate and wise enough to marry a wife with a handsome home and income. The palace is a one-hundred-and-twenty-year-old Gothic revival. It has six bedrooms, four baths, and servants' quarters. Typical of its era, it has fourteen stained-glass windows, a wine cellar, and an annual heating budget that rivals the gross national product of some third world countries. The house sits in the middle of a five-acre park surrounded by a six-foot iron fence.

When my grandparents were alive all five acres were under careful cultivation, but I had given all but a third of an acre up to nature. I could look out the windows of the palace and think about the wild things living inside my fence. Furry folk setting up housekeeping in my grandmother's overgrown maze and herb garden. Most houses like ours had become mortuaries, condos, or had simply been torn down. The families could no longer afford them, or they had scattered and the big houses were no longer needed. I suppose I'd hung on because I could.

Almost as soon as I pressed the remote button to open the gate, I heard the dogs begin to bark. My parents spent over forty years trying to create a new breed of dog. The goal was to combine the British collie types: Aussies, Borders, and roughs, with various retriever types, mostly Labs. Their efforts resulted in Episcopal homes throughout the diocese being filled with good-natured mutts with slightly comical faces. My father always had at least one dog with him wherever he went. I used to tease him that he had successfully bred dogs that could sleep under any desk, in any sacristy.

Meg and Russ were the latest in a long line of keepers. I learned to walk by pulling myself up on Meg's great, great, great, great-grandsire, Robbie. As I was an only child, the dogs had been my sibling substitutes, and I loved them dearly. They had served the same purpose for my daughter. She laughed when she saw them running for the car.

As we climbed out of the car, we were besieged with tails and tongues. Chloe squatted down and started kissing their necks. Russ, the young male, was so overcome with joy he started circling the car and barking. Chloe looked like a happy twelve-year-old sitting on the ground. In a minute or two the dogs settled down, panting, goofy looks on their faces. We were home and their world was complete. Lucky dumb mutts.

'Welcome home, Chloe.' I gave her a hand to pull her up and hugged her to me. 'We'll get your things later. We better check on your grandfather.'

Chloe started up the stairs, and I followed her. At the landing I grabbed her hand to stop her. 'He looks different. He's very thin, and his circulation is shutting down. Talk to him as you normally would, just in case he can hear you.' She nodded her head and opened the door.

This room was my parents' bedroom for their whole married life. When my mother died, no changes were made other than removing her clothes from the closets and drawers. Six months before I'd had the big four poster moved into the basement storage area and brought in a hospital bed. Six months later I hadn't adjusted to the change. The bedroom, like the rest of the house, was filled with Wolden family furniture and carpets. We don't change things, we replace them. I hated the chrome and formica monstrosity that had taken the place of my parents' bed. I even hated the bed linens. Mother had always insisted on beautiful duvets and counterpanes. This bed was covered with cheap cotton blankets that were easy to launder.

He looked so tiny. Never a very big man, he had shrunk to less than one hundred pounds. His silver hair had faded and thinned, its texture brittle. His face was mottled, his hands bluish. That had changed since the morning. Death was quickening its pace. I wished he would die right then and get it over with. I hoped he would never leave me.

Laura sat in an easy chair by the window. She was knitting what seemed like the hundredth sweater since she had arrived three months before. 'It's been a quiet morning.'

'Laura, this is my daughter, Chloe.' Chloe half smiled and nodded in Laura's direction. Normally polite, she was struck dumb by her grandfather's appearance, her first direct look at death.

I leaned over and kissed his brow. 'Dad, Chloe is here. I just picked her up at the airport.' I signaled Chloe over to the bedside.

'Hi, Grandpa, I love you.' She turned, her eyes filling with tears. She looked back at me and shook her head. She couldn't do it, be a part of this, I understood.

'Dad, I'm going to let you rest now. I'll get Chloe some lunch, then I'll be back to say your rosary for you.' I stroked his arm as I spoke to him.

I signaled to Laura, and we all left the room. 'Any changes?' For almost six months my life had been determined by 'changes'.

'You noticed the mottling of course. That will increase. His breathing is much shallower than it's been. I'm still giving the morphine, but I haven't seen any indications of pain. It's almost over. You two all right?' Her question lilted, her accent strong. Laura was my mentor, my guide through the land of the dying. I knew I would miss her when this was over.

'We're fine. Let's go find some lunch, or shall we order something in?' Laura and I had been living on deli, Chinese, and pizza for the last month.

'I have a surprise for you, dear girl. Your fairy godmother has arrived, and she's in the kitchen even as we speak.'

'Hannah? Good old Hannah. She didn't need to come.' Hannah and her husband, George, had been the palace's couple since before I was born. When they retired they moved into an apartment in town and bought an RV. They were usually still in Florida this time of year. Hannah had offered to forgo their yearly migration in the fall, but I declined her offer since she and George had uncertain health themselves.

'She *did* need to come, and you should have asked her sooner. She's in her glory down there banging around pots and complaining about your lousy cleaning lady. George is down there, too, polishing flatware of all things.'

'Come on, Chloe. No effete yuppie food today, pure 'merican food. Laura, why don't you come down for a minute? Wouldn't you like a quick break?' We hurried down the backstairs.

The scene in the kitchen took me back fifteen years. Hannah had her back to us, working over the sink. George was hunched over a tray of silver. He wore a striped apron

I hadn't seen since they'd retired. 'Oh George, Hannah, thank you for coming! I can't tell you how good it is to see you in here.'

Hannah is a big woman, well over two hundred pounds. I hugged her hard, and her size combined with the smells and sights of the kitchen made me feel like a small child. I heard a sound like an injured animal. I realized it was my own sobbing.

'Oh Hannah, I'm sorry. Not much of a welcome.' I was gasping and giggling at the same time. For the past weeks I had seemed always to be close to hysteria. Sometimes I giggled, sometimes I cried, sometimes I did both.

'Don't worry about it, Jilly. How are you holding up, honey? We would have come sooner, but we had the RV down in Florida. You know how George hates the cold now. Well, George said it was way too cold, but I told George he could just wear a coat because Jilly would need all the help she could get.'

George rarely spoke, and I suspected he didn't care where he went. Hannah was always quoting George, but I never knew if she used him to say things she wouldn't or if he talked non-stop when they were alone.

'I'm fine, Hannah. I'm so glad to see both of you.' I turned and smiled at George.

'Chloe, look at you. You are prettier every time I see you. You look more like your daddy every day. You sure don't look like your mama. She was always such a little thing. Just look at you. Come give me a hug. Where are your manners?' She held out her arms and pulled my daughter into her huge bosom, engulfing the girl in aged flesh.

'Hi, Hannah. I'm glad you're here. You look good.' She returned Hannah's embrace, walked over to George, and kissed the top of his head. He smiled up at her.

'Jilly, who is keeping house for you these days? This

place is a disgrace. I haven't been upstairs, but it looks awful down here. Your mother must be rolling over in her grave to see her house like this. I don't expect you to do everything yourself, but you do have to supervise. You have to watch people. You and the Bishop were never any good with help. You have to keep people in line. I've told you all this, and I know your mother told you the same. I heard her myself.'

'Nobody could keep this house the way you did, Hannah. Things went to hell the day you left.' Hannah and I had this discussion every time she set foot in the house. The house looked fine thanks to a crew that came in once a week. Since Hannah's reign, I'd closed off one wing of the house to save on heating and cleaning.

'You didn't answer my question. Who's keeping house?' The question could just as easily have been who let the puppies in the dining room, who took a jar of jam, who cut the fringe off the ottoman. I was seven years old again, and I had better come clean.

'I use a service. They send in a crew of five people, and they do it all in about two hours. I do the laundry and cooking myself. If I need something special, I call Jenny Brady. It works for me.' I shrugged and looked aside. Judas Priest, forty-three years old and still explaining myself to Hannah.

'A service? I hope you have counted the silver, missy. Your mother is turning over in her grave.'

'Hannah, mother was cremated. No grave, no turning over.' I knew she was old, I knew she meant well, but that day I had my own sack of rocks to drag around.

'You always had a fresh mouth. I told George you would outgrow it, but this time I was wrong. I'm hurt, but I'm not leaving. I'll stay, but not for you Jilly, not for you. I'm staying for your mother. There are going to be a million things to do once the Bishop dies, and no service can handle that. No service in the world can replace professional, loyal staff.' Clearly Hannah was back and having one hell of a good time. Every home has a pecking order and this old hen was laying claim to her bit of the roost.

'Dear, dear Hannah, you are right. Be patient with me. I've been running things by myself too long, and my judgment is cloudy.' I knew from experience that Hannah had no sense of irony. She gave me a beatific smile. I was forgiven. Peace reigned once more.

'Jilly, I'm going upstairs while you eat. Can you spell me for about an hour after your lunch?' Laura asked. I'd forgotten for a minute that we had left Dad alone. Of course he wasn't going anywhere, but I was afraid he might come to, for even a moment, and be alone. I didn't want him to be alone at the end.

'Sure, Laura. Can we bring a tray up to you?' I knew she'd decline, but I always offered. Laura refused to eat in the sickroom. I'd decided it was one of those Irish things.

'No thanks. I'll get something later.' She smiled and left the kitchen.

'She seems nice enough, Jilly. Is she good with your father? We had some good Irish girls here before. I would rather have them than the Eyetalians, and that's the truth.' Hannah had very strong opinions about most ethnic groups.

'Laura has been wonderful. She's been very careful to give Dad as much control as possible over his care. I've learned so much from her. You'd be amazed at what a competent nurse I've become.' Normally squeamish, I had learned to ignore what my eyes saw and what my nose smelled. An extension of the trick that gets a mother through the diapering stage.

'George always said you could do anything you put your mind to. You were always a quick little thing. Too full of yourself, but that wasn't your fault. Your folks thought the sun rose and set by you. More like a princess than anything, they treated you.' Yeah, yeah, some princess. The problem with knowing someone for your whole life is they know where all the hot buttons and all the sore spots are.

'Well, I don't know about everyone else, but I'm starved.' I was rarely hungry, but always eating. As my father grew smaller, I seemed to take each pound he lost and slap it on my hips or thighs. I told myself I was keeping my strength up. Perhaps in the event I would need to move the house off its foundation?

'I got up before light and stewed a chicken. I told George the best flavor is from an old hen. I made your favorite, Jilly. I'll be dead on my feet by three, but I didn't want to let you down.' The cook as martyr. Hannah was always making a huge sacrifice to please some ungrateful, unworthy person. She'd sacrificed the equivalent of seventeen virgins for me alone.

'Chicken pie? You shouldn't have.' She really shouldn't have. It was my favorite as a small child, but I could barely swallow it anymore.

We sat down at the worn kitchen table as Hannah started dishing up lunch. Chloe looked a little green around the gills. Not surprising, considering her condition and her own memories of Hannah's chicken pie. I would eat the damn thing but I wasn't going to force Chloe.

'I think Chloe should just have some herbal tea and some dry toast. She got a little gippy on the plane and probably shouldn't push it.' Chloe looked at me gratefully and started to leave the table.

'You, sit down, Chloe. Let me get it for you, baby. I'm here for as long as you need me and as long as I'm here this is my kitchen.' Hannah enjoyed someone feeling under the weather. If I'd needed a mustard plaster her day would have been complete. She banged around happily, a non-verbal indication that nothing was in its proper place.

'Thanks, Hannah. Is there any wheat bread, seven grain, anything like that?' Chloe was very careful about her diet. I wished she had been very careful about everything else. God, I didn't even know who the father was. The last time I asked about such things she wasn't seeing anyone special. He was special now. The father of my grandchild, if it became a child. It was only a short time ago I'd realized I would never have another baby myself, and now I was going to be a grandmother. If it became a child. When I found I was pregnant with Chloe, she was already a baby, a child in my mind and heart.

'Jilly, I think you'd better come up now.' Laura's voice was loud and tinny through the old intercom.

I pressed the lever down just long enough to say one word: 'Coming'. Laura wouldn't have called me if it wasn't the end. 'Come on Chloe.'

I took Chloe's hand, and we walked quickly out of the kitchen and down the hall. I could hear Hannah saying something to us, but the words didn't register. They faded as the blood pounded in my ears. Chloe squeezed my hand and pulled me along, her long legs forcing me almost to run up the backstairs.

'I'm glad you got here in time.' We stopped at the open door, and I hugged her to me. 'Laura?'

'Come here, Jilly.' Laura was leaning over his bed, stroking his hand.

She drew aside his sheet and showed me his legs. Already reduced by disease to bone and stretched skin, they had turned a mottled purple. Laura had explained to me several days before that this was one of the final changes. She also cupped her ear toward the bed, indicating I should listen. His breath rattled with long pauses between intakes.

'I'll leave you three alone now. I'm right outside the door. Goodbye, you darling man.' She kissed my father's hand, patted me on the shoulder, and stepped into the hall.

Death is one of the two experiences we all share but have little contact with. Not too long ago, by the time people reached adulthood they had stood at several deathbeds. By the same token, a girl might have seen several births before she became a mother herself. Birth and death are now managed by professionals, hidden away, cleaned up. Births are speeded by drugs and surgeries. Death is slowed by the same methods.

Death wasn't a complete stranger. I was familiar with the aftermath. I had dutifully attended dozens of funerals and memorials. My husband's death on the thruway was without warning, without mercy. Cremation had been a necessity. My mother had died in the hospital at night when I was home with my daughter. She'd felt viewing was barbaric, and I happily honored her wishes. At funerals and wakes with open caskets, I had always managed to look above the body, to slip out of the room if need be. I had never looked directly at death. Now I was its hostess, its handmaiden.

Dad had said a number of times that death was the last great adventure. The older and sicker he became, the less he said that. He moved from a desire for adventure to seeking rest and peace. I was sorry he required so many pain killers. He had mentioned once he hoped he would be awake so he wouldn't miss anything.

As a clergyman, death was his business partner. Most people sit in pews because of death, the fear of death. His relationship with death was similar to that of an accountant with the taxman. He had studied near death experiences and witnessed two or three unusual deathbed scenes. He once watched an old, comatose woman sit straight up in bed and say, 'Oh good, you're here,' then crumple back, dead. I recall his saying there was an instant where he felt that something had been yanked out of her body just before she fell back. Of course, as a man of God, he didn't look for such proofs of life after death, but as a romantic he loved to hear about them.

I had planned for weeks what I was going to say. I had rehearsed it in my mind a hundred times. I had even written down several Bible verses and bits from the Book of Common Prayer he might want to hear as he left. He felt sure about his destination but, like many people, I pick and choose my beliefs from several sources.

I sat down on the edge of his bed and took his hand. 'It's time, Dad. You need to go. Follow the light, go and follow the light. I love you, Daddy, forever and ever.' I listened for the next breath, but it never came. I was surprised at how still everything seemed. After months of waiting, death was quiet and unobtrusive. A gentleman.

It was all so simple. The dinner over, the last candle blown out. No angels, no long-dead friends and relatives. I was a little disappointed and wondered if he was. My father was not the only romantic in the family. He was gone. I was no longer a beloved child or a devoted daughter. An orphan, I was the next in line.

I don't know how long I sat there, stroking his hand, patting his arm. I came to no great conclusions. No truths were revealed. For the first time in months there was nothing to do for him, nothing to say.

I had been planning to talk to my father until the mortuary picked him up, in case his soul was sitting in the corner. I wanted him to know he was loved, would be missed. Somehow, words wouldn't come. Silence was called for. Clearly what my father had been was gone. All gone. Gone for good.

Chloe leaned against the wall, tears traveling down her cheeks. She stared at the bed with expressionless eyes. My father had been the only father Chloe could remember. All the men died on her, one way or another.

'You need to say goodbye to him. You'll be sorry if you don't.'

She walked to the foot of the bed and touched his blanket covered foot. 'Goodbye, Grandpa. I wish I had . . .'. She sobbed and covered her face.

I pulled her to me, and we walked toward the door.

'Laura? Oh, there you are.' Laura stood leaning against the wall a few feet from the doorway.

She came toward us and hugged me for a moment. 'You kept him home, and that's what he wanted, Jilly. You did a great job. I hope you know that.' I did know. It just didn't seem like very much.

'I can't believe it's finally over. Laura, will you call the mortuary and Mary for me? I'm afraid I'll lose it if I get on the phone.' For the first time I realized my face was wet, my nose running.

'I'll take care of everything. You two go into your room and rest. Do you want anything?'

'Nothing, thank you. How about you, Chloe? Tea, something?' She shook her head.

I put my arm around Chloe's waist, and she put hers around my shoulder. Several doors down the hall we turned into my sitting room. Chloe curled her long legs onto the window seat. It didn't seem too many years ago she was too short to get on the seat without help. I sat on the sofa in front of the cold fireplace. I thought about making a fire, but it seemed like too much work. I wiped my face with my sleeve. Getting a tissue seemed like too much work as well.

Months ago, Dad had planned for this afternoon. He had made a list of names and telephone numbers and given it to his long-time secretary, Mary Arnold. Although she had retired from the diocese when my father did, she had remained with him on a part-time basis. She had agreed that, on receiving word of my father's death, she would call everyone on the list and notify them of the arrangements. Before she did this, she would call the cathedral to set the time and date of the memorial mass. He had also made arrangements with the mortuary for immediate cremation with internment of the ashes in the Wolden crypt with my mother, their two stillborn sons, and my husband Rick.

I hoped I would be able to sleep. I wouldn't need to get up to give injections or comfort. I would have that awful bed picked up. The linens should be tossed out, the room aired. The dogs could come upstairs again. I could do what I wanted again. I was sorry I had never smoked. I wanted to blow smoke out of my nose and mouth as the last few months fell into the past, his and mine.

'What do you think my chances are of getting a beer without going to the kitchen? I don't want to see anybody yet, especially Hannah.' A beer, a dark beer would taste great. It would taste even better if I didn't have to move off the sofa.

'I'll get it. Do you want anything else, something to eat? Chicken pie?' Chloe smiled mischievously.

'No food, but bring me two bottles of the dark beer. Just in case the first one tastes as good as I think it will. And oh, bring the dogs up. We definitely need dogs.'

Chloe patted me on the head as she walked toward the door. I had told her we would talk about the pregnancy, but I couldn't do that yet. There was too much to tell her, too many important things. Today I just wanted to drink beer and sit in my favorite room. I wanted to pet my dogs, hug my daughter, maybe cry, maybe laugh. I didn't want to talk, not about that at least.

I got up and went into my bathroom to wash my face and rinse my contact lenses. I stripped off my skirt and sweater and pulled on old jeans and a heavy fisherman-knit sweater. I put thick wool socks on my feet, which felt like they were made of ice. April in New England can be very cold, and the sky was beginning to cloud over. I didn't intend to see anyone today. I didn't care how I looked. I undid the roll of hair at the nape of my neck and ran my fingers hard against my scalp. I watched my reflection as I braided my graying hair, surprised the day hadn't changed my face.

A loud bang at the door announced Meg and Russ. Because Dad had become so fragile, the dogs hadn't been allowed upstairs since before Christmas. When I opened the door, they looked half-mad with joy. I scratched their necks and patted their flanks. They sniffed and rubbed against the furniture to re-establish their claim on the room. Chloe walked in a moment later with a covered tray.

'How's everything downstairs?' I'd forgotten there were probably people in the chapel and nobody had spoken to Hannah and George.

'Hannah's crying, George is polishing. Hannah wants to talk to you, but I said you were resting. She insisted on sending up the chicken pie. I did grab some other stuff. I found some pasta salad and a frittata or something.' She placed the tray on a gateleg table next to the fireplace.

'Thanks. I'm in no hurry to talk to Hannah or anyone but you and Laura. Let's make that the rule today. You and I are prostrate with grief and will only communicate through Laura.' I opened a beer and savored the dark cold liquid.

'Sounds like a plan. Give this to the dogs?' She held up the pan of chicken pie.

'Sure. Oh shit, somebody is coming.' I heard the heavy tread of feet in the hallway.

'The guys from the mortuary. I saw the hearse pull up when I was downstairs.' She made it sound very ordinary. The electrician is here, the plumber just left; the mortician is here, the caterer just called. I wondered if my daughter lacked the grief gene or simply had an overdose of resilience.

'That was fast. I'm sure Laura will handle it. Who let them in?' I could be resilient too. I would be so glad when things returned to normal. For weeks my home had been invaded with people I didn't know. I would never take privacy for granted again.

'Some beautiful priest who was in the chapel. He offered to take care of the door and the gate. I told him to check with Laura if he had any questions.'

'Good girl. How are you doing?' I took another swallow of the beer, hoping I hadn't opened Pandora's box.

'Okay. Maybe it hasn't hit me yet. In some ways this sounds awful, but the last couple of years he hasn't been a big part of my life. That's not quite what I mean. I don't know what I mean. I think I'm so worried about myself – I'm sorry.' She turned away.

'I wanted to put you off a while longer. I don't know why. I guess I hope this will go away if we ignore it. I always hoped this would never happen to you. I really believed that by my being open and honest about sex and birth control you would have an edge. Of course all that is neither here nor there. You need to make some plans, and I'd like to help you do that.' I hadn't looked at her during my short speech. Somehow this was my fault. Good mothers didn't have pregnant eighteen-year-old daughters. Good mothers didn't become grandmothers in their mid-forties, at least not in this neighborhood.

'If it makes you feel any better I was using a contraceptive. It didn't work. The damn thing just didn't work.' Chloe was sitting back on the window seat, scratching the top of Russ's head.

'Who is the man?' The sixty-four-thousand-dollar question. I hadn't asked before for fear she would tell me she didn't know. I was afraid he was a dreadlocked Rastafarian, a married Rotarian, a Moslem falafel chef.

'That's not important, at least not now. I haven't told him anything. I'm not sure I ever will.'

'I think it's very important. He has a right to know and frankly, so do I.' An only child, she was selfish with toys and information.

'It's not important because I'll probably have an abortion. It would be stupid for me to even consider having a baby right now.' I could barely hear her. She was almost mumbling. An old trick from her pre-teens, mumbling what was really on her mind. It was an excellent device for avoiding and at the same time inviting conflict. Everything was thrown into the adult's court.

'If you decide to abort, I won't stop you.' A lie. 'Perhaps it is the best thing to do under the circumstances. However, I don't believe you really want that. If you wanted an abortion, you could have had one. I would never have known. You could have kept me out of this completely, but you didn't. You must have some reason for pulling me into this.'

'I told you because you guessed. I wouldn't have come home this break, but I had to because of Grandpa. I never would have told you if you hadn't guessed. I still can't believe this has happened. The weird thing is, as much as I hate the fact I'm pregnant, I can't help but be excited. I don't know anything about babies. I obviously can't take care of myself, much less a baby. My field work starts in July in a Mexican slum for Christ's sake! God I wish I were a guy. They climb out of bed and say, "love ya babe", leave and start all over.'

'Tell me about him.' I thought she wanted to tell me. I knew I wanted to know.

'I just did. As we speak he is in Palm Springs, probably watching a wet tee-shirt contest and sucking on his fifth long-neck Corona. This morning he most likely crawled out of bed and said, "love ya babe". The frat boy's mantra. I wish

I could tell you I fell in love with his mind, but I didn't. Are you shocked?'

'Shock is too strong a term. I'm surprised, but I'd like to know more. I'd like to know a little more about him.' I'd like to know a lot more about this kid who had changed Chloe's life. One shot of sperm, one successful polliwog, and my daughter's personal history is rewritten. And he is in Palm Springs, the little fucker. Low-life sperm bank with acne and dirty fingernails.

'His name is Will. I met him about two months ago at a party. He's a senior, pre-med. He grew up in Park City, Utah. His family is tied in with some resort. He's the youngest of three, the only boy. He's very good looking. He comes across as one of those Phil Donahue, nineties kind of men. God, I'm a wonderful judge of character.'

'Actually, Chloe, if you haven't told him, if he doesn't know, what do you expect in the way of response? Maybe you need to cut him some slack.' Of course I was ready to rip his heart out and eat his liver raw. Perhaps while she cut him some slack, I could rip off his arm and beat him with it.

'Maybe I'm just pissed I'm pregnant. I'm sick, I'm screwed, and he's not. I hope I never see him again.'

'Did either of you give any thoughts to AIDS? What about safe sex? I'm almost more concerned about that than pregnancy. Not to be harsh, but what were you thinking about?' My voice had risen and I fought for control. Kids think they are immortal.

'Give me some credit, Mother. We both had a test six weeks ago, and we are both in low-risk groups. He hadn't had sex for about six months, and I hadn't been with anyone for almost four.' Chloe recited this so casually. I think I would rather have died than discuss my sex life with my mother. I left notes rather than ask my mother to buy pads and tampons for me.

'Chloe, I don't want to lecture you. I want you to realize though that whatever you decide will be with you forever. You need to be sure about whatever you do.'

'Right now I just want to sleep. I was on the red-eye last night, and I feel like my eyelids are made of sandpaper. Could we talk about this later, maybe even tomorrow?' She looked tired and disheveled. She reminded me of one of those kids you find sleeping in airports, waiting for stand-by flights.

'Of course. Your room is ready, and you can sleep as long as you want. I'd suggest you turn off the bell to your phone. Lots of calls will be coming in, and you don't need to be bothered.' We hugged for a moment, and she went out the door.

I lit the gas logs in the fireplace. It didn't put out any real heat but I felt warmer anyway. I debated leaving my room and checking on Laura and Mary, but Chloe wasn't the only one suffering from lack of sleep. For weeks I had been daydreaming about having nothing to do. Now I couldn't relax and enjoy it.

The response to grief is as varied as hair color. My response has always been one of frenzied activity. When Rick died, I threw myself into settling his affairs, caring for Chloe, and doing volunteer work. When my mother died, I had the house repainted and replaced all the window coverings and much of the upholstery. This was not a day for sitting still, as much as I might want to. Other people could handle everything, but everything was my responsibility.

I found Laura in my father's room, counting vials of medication and making notations. The bed was already stripped, two bulging garbage bags on the floor.

'Laura? It looks like you've got everything under control.' I was a little disappointed. I needed something to do.

'I'm just finishing a bit of paperwork. The rental place

should pick up the bed in just a bit. The phone's been ringing off the hook, but Mary is here to handle that. Your friend Susan is on her way. I told her you weren't seeing anyone today, but she insisted. She said you could kick her out if you wanted but she was coming.' She only looked up briefly from her notes and vials.

'You're a wonder, Laura. I'll call down to Mary that Susan can come up when she gets here. I can't tell you how much I appreciate everything you did for Dad, and for me. I don't know what we would have done without you.'

'I've enjoyed being here. I'm going to take a couple days off before I take another assignment so I'll be at the service.'

'Good. There is going to be a reception after the service back here. I hope you will come for that too.' I made a note to tell Mary to add Laura's name. I had planned for a brief reception at the cathedral with an invitation-only luncheon in the early afternoon.

'Thank you, I'll be here. This just about takes care of it.' Laura was gathering her papers and medicine into a large canvas tote.

'I almost forgot. This is from Dad.' I handed her a long white envelope.

'What's this?'

'It's a check. Dad wanted you to have something in addition to your agency pay.'

'Thank you. You shouldn't have, but I'm glad you did.' She looked inside the envelope. 'I'm really glad you did.' The check was for three thousand dollars.

'Have some fun with it. You earned every penny of it.' The intimacy of death was gone, and I was sad to realize she was, and had been all along, hired help.

As I headed downstairs, I heard someone coming up the backstairs. Turning around I saw Susan step into the hall.

Susan had been my best friend since we were nine years old. She is the closest thing I've ever had to a sister. These last few years she is also the closest thing I've had to a mother. Susan has had six children and tends to treat everyone as though they were child number seven. Susan is an L.L. Bean Madonna with a Range Rover.

'Am I ever glad to see you.' I kissed her cheek and got a whiff of soap and powder, perhaps a hint of gingerbread?

'I came as soon as I heard. Mary said Chloe made it in time?' Chloe is Susan's godchild. One of many. Susan probably has as many godchildren as Princess Diana.

'God, Susan. He's gone.' I leaned against her. 'When I picked up Chloe I found out she was pregnant. What timing. I don't know what to say to her.'

'Well, for starters it's time to tell her how her situation is not unique. I think she needs to be told everything.' Susan was never one to mince words.

CHAPTER TWO

'Keep your voice down for the love of God! Chloe is in her room.' I could hear the hiss in my voice and regretted it. I signaled Susan into my room.

'Sit down, Jilly. Take a minute to collect yourself.' One of the nice things about Susan is she does know when to shut up. She sat me down on the sofa, went behind me, and started rubbing my temples.

'Christ, that feels good. Would you do my neck? I feel like it's full of cement.' Susan has great hands, long fingers, short nails.

'Settle down and relax. There is not a thing you can do about anything right now. Just take it easy, and don't talk until you're ready.'

'Susan, everything is so huge all of a sudden. I like the ordinary, the pedestrian. I'm not equipped to watch my surviving parent die on the same day my unmarried child tells me she is pregnant. Where is Oprah when you need her?'

'It's all pretty rotten, Jill. You don't have to be a rock right now. I hope you know that. Just let me take care of things. Mary is handling all the arrangements for your father, so you don't have to think about that.' Susan was cheerful, knowing her talents and skills were being used.

'I was ready for Dad. He was ready. I was ready. I'm really not even sad. It's weird, but it's not really sad. I really think he's been gone for a few days anyway. His heart just took a while to stop beating. But I just can't believe Chloe is pregnant! How could she do this to me? Now of all times. Why can't things ever happen one at a time?'

'Girls get pregnant all the time. Hell, I get pregnant all the time. Did you know she was sexually active? Was that a surprise?'

'I knew, but I also knew she was careful, very careful. Last semester she was an AIDS counselor in her dorm. She was the one passing out condoms, for Christ's sake.'

'How does she feel about the pregnancy? Is she angry, sad? What is she feeling?'

'She feels like not talking for the most part. Apparently the father is some frat boy who is in Palm Springs for break. She hasn't even told him about the baby. Isn't that odd? Talking about a baby. I shouldn't call it a baby. It will probably never be a baby. The idea of killing a fetus disgusts me.' *There, I said it.*

'I'm surprised, I always thought you were pro-choice. I know you are pro-choice. We've discussed this before.' We had argued about it several times. Susan felt every scrap of tissue was precious, and I was convinced every woman had a right to decide what to do with her uterus, grow geraniums in it for all I cared.

'I am pro-choice. I think every woman has a right to choose. But this is my grandchild. It has a right to live. This is my baby, too; it's Rick's baby. I say that, but I don't want Chloe to be a mother right now. I know she's not ready. She knows she's not ready. Shit, piss, hell, fuck, and shit!' I shot the words out like bullets, surprised they didn't leave smoking holes in the worn chintz of the slipcovers.

'Fine talk for the Bishop's daughter.' Susan threw a small

pillow at me, and we both started laughing. Nothing was funny, but laughing cleared some of the tension.

'You really need to talk to her, let her know how you feel.' Susan seemed to believe I would never think this out by myself.

'I realize that. Obviously I'll talk to her, but this has to be her decision. I know what happens. Everybody knows what's best except for the poor scared kid. Once an egg is fertilized, a girl becomes public property. I won't let that happen to my daughter.' Even if she was a stupid, careless, oversexed twit with the world's worst timing.

'I really don't know what I would do, how I would feel. I wouldn't abort of course. Poor Chloe. Eighteen is so young to deal with this. Even you were twenty, and I remember how awful it was for you.' Susan gave me her most sympathetic look, and I was tempted to kick her well-loved butt out of the door. I'm cursed with a best friend who is kind, charming, beautiful, happily married, and is still a perfect size ten. If I didn't love her so much, I would hate her.

'God, don't remind me. The best girl in the world, the apple of her Daddy's eye. Sometimes, Susan, I think I've lived the last twenty-three years trying to prove that I'm not a slut. Do you know, I'm still afraid people will find out?'

The terror I had felt at twenty was still fresh in my mind. I ignored the pregnancy for two months. I was naïve. Perhaps I thought it would go away. Perhaps I could pray it away. Killing myself wasn't an option. It would have embarrassed my parents horribly. Chloe wasn't going to have to go through that at least.

'Jilly, I think you are a wonderful person. You've always been a wonderful person. I never felt the same about your parents afterwards, I must admit. There is no reason why you couldn't have kept the baby.' The Susans of the world didn't give away babies.

'I was never angry with them. I was angry with myself

that I didn't fight them, but I understood how they felt, I understood how Borden felt as well. I simply didn't know I would never, ever stop wanting that baby back.' Susan is so patient. I must have said this to her a hundred times through the years. The litany of the birth mother.

'Kip Borden shouldn't have been a factor in your keeping the baby. It should have been your decision. Did I tell you I saw Kip a few weeks ago?' I hadn't seen Kip in ten years, but he still weaves just outside my life.

'We saw him down in Hilton Head. I pretended I didn't see him. I spoke to his wife briefly. She looks more like a baseball player's wife every time I see her. There should be a law about being perky after the age of thirty-five.' Susan understands that best friends hate the same people.

We laughed, enjoying the process of mocking the enemy. It has always been easier to hate her rather than him. Why do women reserve their strongest negative emotions for other women? Is it because we expect better of each other?

Did I expect Wendy to toss aside her engagement so I could marry Kip? Did I expect Kip to marry me with the understanding we could divorce once the baby was born? Of course I did. I will hate them forever and ever, amen.

Kip Borden was the person who completely reordered my life. With the help of wine from his father's cellar and skin that smelled of Kanoe, I lost my virginity accompanied by Simon & Garfunkel. In spite of the aftermath, I still love the smell of Kanoe and the sound of Simon & Garfunkel.

We went to the Bordens' summer house on the Cape in November. We told each other we were studying for finals, but in those days that's what young, would-be lovers said, even to each other.

Even then, we were beginning to realize we were of a dying breed. Immigrants come and adapt to a new life. As they adapt, they make major changes in themselves. They also make minor changes in society. Through the years, change piles on, shifts occur, some grow, some die. In the late sixties, with the attention to racial diversity and racial prejudice, people began to look for and take pride in their ethnic and racial identities. At the same time, history was being rewritten to make many of the things we had held dear seem cruel, ugly, and stupid in the light of the latter part of the twentieth century.

People like Kip and I found we were the direct inheritors of a way of life that seemed quite tarnished. Our trust funds were often the result of practices better left unexamined. The WASP was quickly losing its sting. Many of us began to socialize within a very narrow sphere. We dated people from familiar schools, familiar clubs. The barbarian was at the gate, and we would hold our own as long as we could. This was about the time my mother put the electric security gate across the old iron fence that surrounded our home. The fence and gate, designed to keep the dogs in, now served a new purpose. I have often wondered if mother considered it to be a success.

Kip's mother was in the Junior League with mine. I had known him since we were ten. I don't remember him at that age, I just know our paths did cross. We dated briefly in our sophomore year, but we didn't go to the Cape for another year. I wasn't in love with him, but I did feel a need for direction and purpose. I hoped if I could love him, perhaps marry him, my life would have order.

I never tried to trap him. I certainly didn't try to become pregnant to force him into marriage. If a marriage took place before graduation, everyone counted the months. At that time it was important to maintain every appearance of virginity. Actually most of the girls I knew were virginal even if they were not quite virgins.

Romance did not bloom that cold weekend on the

Cape. We were clumsy and wanted to be in love to justify our actions. My passion quickly changed to embarrassment and resentment for his part in my actions. I remember being concerned he would tell his friends, ruin my reputation. I had already changed my opinion about myself and didn't want others to do the same.

I'll never know how he felt. Within a few days he was dating a beautiful girl from the West Coast. If his intention was to find the opposite to me he succeeded. She was tall and willowy, blonde and billowy. In my mind she was a cheerleader, but I don't know if she was in fact. She would have made a damned fine cheerleader. I like to think she still has pom-poms in a trunk. I do know Kip was mad about her. They were engaged about a week before I realized I was pregnant.

I thought about an abortion, but since abortion was illegal and, for all intents and purposes, unavailable, I never gave it serious consideration. I'd heard about a girl dying, bleeding to death in her dorm room while her roommate watched a football game. You didn't need to be religious to see this as the wages of sin. She didn't deserve to die, but she'd asked for it, nonetheless.

Even a short-term marriage was out of the question. It would have been my first choice, but Kip told me he would deny the child was his and find other men who would say they had slept with me. Kip told me to get rid of it and not call him back. Kip is now a prominent state Senator and vehemently pro-life. He has two daughters and I bet they are both cheerleaders.

I remember sitting in my father's study. I told them in as few words as possible. I was dry eyed and my voice was somehow without tremor. My heart was beating so hard I remember thinking I would die then of a heart attack and everything would be solved. I could join my little blue brothers in the crypt. My parents would mourn me terribly, but my father would be a shining example of how faith could overcome adversity. My mother would amaze everyone with her quiet self control and dignity.

The clock ticked and a dog snored. No other sound. They neither spoke, nor looked at me. After what seemed hours of silence, but was probably only minutes, my father began to speak while my mother nodded in agreement. As though they had discussed this before, they were of one mind.

I would tell my friends I was going to England to study through the spring and summer. I would, in fact, go to England, but to the convent house of the Little Sisters of Mary. I would wait out my time, and the child would be given in adoption to a fine family. I would return to school, and no one would be the wiser. I could go on, knowing that my child was in a loving, Christian home. Someday I would marry and have children. Clean as a whistle, neat as a pin. No anger. No screaming. Dad was on the phone to England before I left the room.

I was so relieved. This thing meant nothing to me but swollen breasts and nausea. Shame and humiliation. My sin was so great a few months on my knees in an Anglican convent was what I needed.

I went back to school for less than a day. My mother helped me pack the few things I needed for the coming months. There was no tension between us as we drove to the airport. I think we all almost believed I really was merely studying abroad for a few months. I kissed my mother goodbye with promises to write every week.

The Little Sisters made their home in a fine old manor house outside Bath. Many of the sisters joined the order after being wives and mothers. Most of the sisters were over fifty, the youngest being in her mid-thirties. As the youngest resident, and the pregnant daughter of an American bishop, I quickly became a favorite.

This convent house, unlike some, was not a home for wayward girls. I was there as a paying guest, but treated as a daughter or younger sister. My pregnancy was a welcome novelty which helped many of the sisters relive their own pregnancies. I was given much advice about my changing body, and the announcement of my baby's quickening was greeted with much delight.

For the first time in years I was around young children. Children and grandchildren were welcome to visit every weekend and they came in droves to picnic and play in the grounds. For the first time in my life, I played with children as an adult. Before the convent, I had never changed a diaper, given a bottle, held a sleeping child.

Within a short time, I fell in love with my baby. The sisters didn't find my pregnancy a source of embarrassment. I no longer tried to hide my shape. I invited others to feel the kicking. I decided I would return home after the delivery with my baby. I would tell everyone his father had died in Vietnam. I would tell them he was a Martian. I would keep my baby.

At twenty, you can still have the magical thinking of childhood. If you say it, if you write it, it will happen. I felt my parents would see my resolve and welcome us back. There would be adjustments, but they would grow to love my baby as much as I did.

I wrote my parents a long, thoughtful letter. I told them I would transfer to a school on the Coast if need be. I could return in a few years with my child and a story. Perhaps I would even return with a husband. I would be a fine mother to their grandchild. I would keep my baby.

My father wrote that after much discussion between them, after much prayer, they had decided the child must be given up for adoption. I was young and didn't understand all the ramifications. A wonderful family was waiting for my baby. I could get on with my life. Although I was not without funds, all of my money was held in trust, with my mother as trustee, they gently reminded me. This was certainly the best and only option. I continued to be foremost in their prayers.

In my eighth month, I was visited by the man I would eventually marry. Rick was an attorney with the firm my mother's family had used since the continents were one. He was vacationing in England and had agreed to check on me and see I had everything I needed. When I told him of my determination to keep the baby, I realized he had been sent to reinforce my parents' wishes. I made him leave, but he returned the next day, and the next. His vacation over, he returned to the States, but he arrived in Bath the day after my son was born.

The hospital refused to let me hold or see the baby. I was not allowed out of my bed and may have been sedated. My memory may not be reliable. I felt like a trapped animal.

When Rick arrived, I begged to hold the baby. I heard Rick's voice down the hall, cajoling, then threatening. He brought me my baby and laid him in my arms.

I held him and cried onto his downy head. He began to wake, and I opened my gown to give him my breast. Rick pulled my gown closed and took the baby from me. He was crying as he clutched my son, unhappy with his part in this. He promised to give me a baby I could keep. He told me he would give me as many babies as I wanted, but I had to give this one away. At least I think he said that. I signed the papers and married Rick a year later. He gave me only one baby. We didn't have time for more.

The dogs started stirring and the door opened slightly. 'Mom, can I come in?' Chloe put her head in the door. Her hair was wet, tied back in a small ponytail. Her face was shiny and pink from a shower.

'Chloe, you lovely thing, come here!' Susan patted the seat next to her.

'How are you Aunt Susie? I'm glad you're here. What's going on, Mom?' She sat next to Susan and held her hand.

'Not much. I haven't gone downstairs yet. I should go over a few things with Mary, but I'm sure she has everything under control.'

'How are you feeling, Chloe? Your mother told me, I hope you don't mind.' It would never occur to Susan her timing was off.

'I don't mind, but if it's all right with everybody I don't want to talk about it. I was thinking while I showered that somehow I've stolen Grandpa's thunder. I want to get through the next few days without thinking about my uterus or its contents. The service and the luncheon, everything, is going to be enough to deal with.' Chloe played with the ends of wet hair as they escaped from the band holding her hair.

'That sounds fine, honey. We'll shelve this until everything has settled down around here.' I was grateful for a reprieve. 'With that in mind, why don't you catch up with Susan while I check in with Mary? There must be a ton of things I need to start chopping away at.' Please God, keep me busy for the next few days. 'I'll see you both in a while.' I tried not to run out of the door.

I found Mary in my father's study. She was on the telephone but signaled for me to sit down across from her. I had no idea who she was talking to, but I heard her crisp announcement of my father's death, along with date and time of the funeral. I didn't realize a date had been set until just then. She finished the call and set the phone down.

'Everything is set for Saturday at ten. Bishop Mark will be by in about an hour to go over the details of the service. The caterer has been notified, and I will have menu selections for you this evening or tomorrow morning. The florist wants you to stop by tomorrow morning. I have a list of messages for you that have come in within the last few hours. If you could take a look at them and tell me which ones you want to return personally, I'll get to the rest as soon as possible.' Mary's religion was efficiency. She loved lists and files.

I glanced at the small pile she had handed me and took two off the top. 'Does Elliott know Dad is gone? I probably should have called him myself.' Elliott was a widower friend of mine. He had been my escort for several months – a term I preferred to stud muffin.

'He was one of the first people I called. He said to let him know what you want him to do. If he doesn't hear from you, he'll stop by this evening.' Mary checked something off a list.

'Sounds good. I wish I didn't have to deal with Bishop Mark, but I guess I won't have to much longer. Has he said anything about the two women who will be serving?' Bishop Mark, who replaced my father ten years earlier, is opposed to women in the priesthood. The Episcopal church dealt with this several years ago, but Bishop Mark, and a few others, still forbade women to function as priests in their dioceses.

'He hasn't said anything yet, and he's had the instructions for the service about three months now. I wouldn't be surprised if he fights you on it. He may not have wanted to argue with your father about it, but the gloves could come off for you. On the other hand he may tell anyone that mentions it that the women are serving as deacons, not as priests. He will be concerned about setting a precedent. After all, he has spent ten years creating a conservative diocese. He won't want to lose that.' Mary was a thirty-year veteran of church politics.

'What happens, happens. I'm not going to argue with him, but I won't hesitate to move the service to St Swithin's, and I'll tell him that. That man makes the Pope look like

Jimmy Swaggert. I'm sick to death of him and his minions. I would prefer the service to be at the Cathedral, that's what Dad wanted, but I won't let him take this over.' My father and I started attending St Swithin's shortly after he retired. It was one of the few parishes in the diocese where liberal and mainstream Episcopalians were still welcome. 'Oh, call the florist, please, and tell him that he can come to me. I've been a great customer for years and I expect some accommodation.'

'I already told the florist it would behoove him to work that into his schedule. He grumbled, but we can always find another florist. Should I call St Swithin's and make tentative arrangements?

'Not yet. No sense in getting our panties in a bunch before we know if there is a problem or not. Whenever I get worked up beforehand, things seem to work out fine. It's when I least expect things I get blind-sided.' Pregnancy for instance. There's a neck-snapper for you.

'We need to talk about the luncheon. The caterer will provide waiters, but we are going to need some extra people in over the next few days to get everything ready. Your mother-in-law and her husband will arrive tomorrow.'

'Oh goody, goody. We're having some fun now.' Before he died, Rick's mother and I fell into a classic mother-in-law, daughter-in-law situation, and we never pulled out of it. She was impressed he was marrying a Wolden until she got to know me. Eleanor was one of those nouveau middle-class country club types, always talking about 'class', which she seemed to think was something she could buy at Bloomingdale's. She thought I was a mousey snob, and she was probably right. We did agree that Chloe was wonderful, however, and maintained the appearance of a relationship for her sake.

Actually, I've known a large number of Eleanor Parkhursts in my time. I've even become friends with some of them. A few years ago I realized I hated Eleanor because I couldn't bear to hate Rick or his memory. He made sure Eleanor never found out about my son. It took me a while to realize he was instrumental in my son's adoption, not just to protect my family, but to protect his as well. I still believe he fell in love with me but he also fell in love with the whole package; the respect, prestige, and money that surrounded me. Like a child eager to please, he laid me at his mother's feet, as he had his excellent grades and his degrees from Yale. I was one of her rewards for successful mothering. Rick wanted his offering to be without blemish, certainly without child.

I loved Rick, the life we had. I didn't speculate on what would have happened if he'd lived. I remembered that brief time of love, passion, youth. I didn't allow it to age.

'Well, you knew she would come. We'll put them in your parents' bedroom, Chloe will be a diversion. I think they are only staying two nights, so that shouldn't be too bad.'

'You're right, of course. I really do wish we could get along better. I always feel on the spot with her. She pries, she clings, she chatters non-stop. She insists on keeping up this charade of the happy extended family.' Eleanor brought out the very worst in me. When she was around I didn't like myself. I became sharp and aloof. She was one of the few people in the world with whom I had a difficult time being pleasant. Eleanor and Bishop Mark. 'Damn, the next few days are going to be fun. Promise me you will throw cold water on me if I get too nasty with Eleanor or His Purpleness.'

'Frankly, Jill, I'm going to leave the room whenever either of those two are around. I've got enough of my own baggage without watching you sling yours around. I'm your father's secretary, not your therapist.' Mary gave me a stern look over the top of her glasses.

'Enough said. I will be an adult and a lady. That should throw everybody for a loop. Now, you said something about extra people? Let's give Jenny a call, and we can ask the agency to send somebody over. Whatever you want is fine with me.'

'Fine. I'll make the calls as soon as we're done. I hope Hannah won't be too much of a pain. She does love to take charge.' Mary and Hannah had locked horns before. Hannah felt running the house included running its occupants.

'Let me deal with Hannah or ignore her. She thinks she is doing us a great favor by being here, and I would like to maintain the illusion. She really does mean well, and at least she knows where everything is in the kitchen.' Everything in the kitchen and everything in the closets.

'This may not be the time, but would you like me to stay on to help with your books and correspondence? On a very part-time basis, of course.'

'Absolutely. Let's not make any changes for a while. I remember what it's like after a death. There will be so many loose ends and things to see about. You're much better at paperwork than I am. Is that all right with you?' I couldn't remember the last time I had signed a check or balanced a bank statement. In truth, Mary had been keeping the house running for the last six months.

'That's fine. If I have too much time on my hands I'll get into trouble. I'm really not good at this kind of thing, Jill, but you know how much I cared for your father, how much I care for you. You have all meant so much to me. I don't really think of myself as an employee, not after all these years.'

'Oh Mary, you are part of the family, you know that.' I walked around the desk, leaned over, and held her. 'You have done so much for both of us these last few months. There were so many things I didn't have to think about because I knew you would take care of them. I can't really remember a time without you.'

'I'm glad I can still keep you on track.' Clearly embarrassed by my affection, she reached for a stack of papers and began sorting them. She often shuffled papers when she felt conversations were interfering with her work, or invading her privacy.

Mary had been widowed for over twenty-five years. After two miscarriages, she and her husband had adopted a new-born baby girl. Four weeks later, her husband died of a heart attack and the adoption agency removed the baby. In those days, single people weren't allowed to adopt. Mary's baby went to the next couple on the list. Mary knew about my son. When I returned from England I wondered if she hated me for giving away the thing she could never have. At the time I hated myself and assumed everyone shared my opinion.

'Well, my dear, I had better get my bottom in gear and start returning calls. Will you let me know when Smiling Mark arrives?' I have a number of names for the Bishop. I find it a healthy and entertaining way to deal with people I don't like. If I can amuse myself with their nicknames while I talk to them, I'm less likely to get nasty. I may be one of the world's most unpleasant people, but I'm the only one who knows for sure. At least I hope I'm the only one.

'I'll let you know.' She returned to her lists.

Interesting situation. I had been mistress of the house since my mother's death, but now I was the head of the family. Odd. It felt like wearing a dress two sizes too big, but comfortable, nonetheless. I felt like walking through the house, spinning, arms akimbo.

I checked with the nice young priest who had been manning the door and told him that I would be in the living room using the phone, that he should notify Mary when the Bishop arrived. I liked to flirt with young priests, the handsome ones at least. Most of them are so serious and full of their new importance. They are very disconcerted to be flirted with by a bishop's daughter. I'd been doing this since I was about twelve, so I supposed it was time to find some new amusements, something more adult and sophisticated. I did make it a rule never to flirt with older priests, however. An older priest might flirt back, call my bluff, make me uncomfortable. As an only child, I still believed the game was only fun if I made the rules.

As I'd hoped, the living room was empty. I returned two calls to old friends of the family. I stopped after two because talking about the last few weeks made me cry. Strange how self control is linked to the mouth. The way we talk, the way we smile, the way we eat, all reveal how we really feel. Meg and Russell wandered into the room and wriggled from excitement when they discovered me. I sat on the floor to pet them for a while. I read somewhere that petting animals is therapeutic. I needed all the therapy I could get.

'Mrs Parkhurst? Bishop Mark just pulled up. Shall I send him in?' The young priest stopped at the arch leading into the living room. Meg was making rumbling sounds in her throat. Russ sat in my lap. A sixty-five pound cowardly lap dog.

'That's fine, Father. Father what, by the way?' This one had real possibilities. He was blond, so perhaps I could make him blush.

'It's Michael, I mean, Father Michael, Father Michael Blaine. I'll bring the Bishop in now, Mrs Parkhurst.' By now Meg was sniffing his knees.

'Jill, my name is Jill.' He blushed, ten points.

'I'll bring the Bishop in now, Jill.' Nice smile. I wondered how old he was. I would send Chloe down later to find out. He might make a pleasant diversion for her right now. On second thoughts, that was a very bad idea. Chloe didn't need handsome blond diversions at the moment. I thought about getting up but decided to stay on the floor. I was comfortable and felt sheltered by the dogs. Many people found Bishop Mark to be kind, gentle, a true man of God. I always found him to be Machiavellian, almost sinister. He had lovely blue eyes, thin silver hair, a soft voice, and a steely determination. He had a dean, an assistant bishop, several deacons, an archdeacon, and many other subalterns to do his bidding. When things backfired he feigned ignorance and offered assurances and promises of satisfaction.

'Jill, my dear, how are you holding up?' The Bishop was in the archway, giving me his best twinkle-eyed smile. Chubby and plump, a right jolly old monk. The Bishop made sure everyone knew that he had taken voluntary vows of celibacy years ago. He was rumored to be a closet gay, which was interesting considering he prohibited any gay organizations within churches in the diocese. Personally, I could never imagine why the God who created the heavens and earth would concern herself with which set of genitals banged against another.

'It's been a very long day, and I'm glad that it's almost over. Thank you for coming.' I held up my hand for him to shake. Never aggressive, but always protective, Meg growled, daring him to touch me. 'No, Meg. He can't hurt me.' I smiled up at him.

'I wanted to be with you, help in any way that I can. Is your daughter here yet?'

'Yes, she got here not long before Dad died. She's upstairs right now, long flight and all.' Russell had climbed off my lap and was sniffing the Bishop's shoes. The man had cats, so I'm sure they smelled wonderful to the dog. Russ was trying to push the man's foot up with his nose to smell the sole of his shoe. I did nothing to stop him.

'May I sit down?' He indicated the chairs in front of the lit fireplace.

'Of course. Would you like coffee, a sherry? I have a lot of help today, we should take advantage of it. I could get you something to eat.' A gracious hostess.

'A sherry would be fine, Jill, but only if you join me.' Russell stopped worrying the man's shoe and began to snuffle at his hand. The Bishop wiped his hand on the arm of the chair.

'Bishop Mark, today I will join you. Frankly, I'd climb in the damned bottle and swim in it if I could.' I went to the archway and called for the young priest. 'Michael, we're going to have a drink. You're welcome to join us, or I can call down to the kitchen if you're hungry. Make yourself at home. I meant to tell you that earlier.' That was partly for show. I wanted the young priest to be taken care of, but I also wanted the Bishop to know he was the only one I treated badly. Almost the only one. There was my mother-in-law, of course.

Father Michael didn't answer, but held up a coffee cup and plate proving he had already discovered how to get fed and watered in this house. I went to a cabinet and poured two rather large sherries into my grandmother's Waterford glasses. I took a drink of mine, refilled it and returned to the Bishop. I gave him his glass and sat down.

'Here is to Bishop James Olin Young, God bless his sweet soul.' I wanted to sound jaunty. I started crying.

'My dear. This has been a terrible time for you. Your father is at peace now.' He was starting one of the priestly rambles I knew I couldn't bear to hear.

'Just promise me you won't make any changes to the service. I need to know it will be what he wanted. I don't want any changes.' I gulped down the sherry, enjoying the burn. I wanted to be drunk. I wanted to be carried upstairs and tucked into bed. I wanted a father.

'There are considerations, nothing major. Women don't serve in this diocese as priests, for one thing. For another—'

'They will serve, they have served. They served when my father was bishop, and you have had these arrangements in writing for over three months. If you weren't going to honor them, you should have told my father. I knew you would pull something like this.' I gave myself a moment's pleasure by thinking about my foot kicking him in the center of his plump pomposity.

'Jill, please understand my point of view. I have an obligation, a duty—'

'You have an obligation to honor the last wishes of the Bishop Emeritus. If you don't, I will have the service at St Swithin's. You can't afford any more bad publicity, and you would surely get it on this one. I'll see to it.' The Bishop was still in hot water with the College of Bishops over his claims that his conservative brethren represented the one true church.

'I may not have always agreed with your father, but I always respected him. I will honor his wishes, but you must realize I am making exceptions out of respect for his memory, not because I feel threatened by you. I am taking into account how upset you are. I hope you won't be too embarrassed when you remember this conversation. Remember it's the grief and the sherry talking.'

'Thank you. I know you are doing the best thing, for all of us.' I turned away so that he wouldn't see me smile. I hadn't expected him to give in so quickly.

'You have been through a tremendous amount. Would you like me to leave? I'll understand if you want to be alone.' He seemed anxious to leave. I couldn't blame him.

'Actually, I want you to stay. I would like you to say Mass for us. Chloe hasn't been to services since Christmas Eve, and that's entirely too long. Would you mind?' Deep down

I'm a peasant who believes a crucifix will protect me from the dark night. A wafer on the tongue will heal a troubled heart. A sip of wine will solve all problems. Much as I disliked the man, I liked his position, wanted its benefit under my roof.

'I think that's an excellent suggestion. Why don't you come into the chapel with me? We'll have Father Michael round everyone up.' He put his arm around my shoulder and led me toward the chapel.

The chapel pre-dates the house's promotion to palace. My great-great-grandfather included the tiny chapel in his house plans more for architectural reasons than religious ones. It has only three pews and can hold a dozen worshippers. The attempt was to duplicate a castle chapel of the Gothic era, but the only things captured were the dark and the dank. The ceiling, walls, and altar were dark, hand-carved walnut, bespeaking a time of cheap labor.

I curled into a corner of a pew watching the bishop go through the familiar housekeeping of preparing for Mass. Chloe, Mary, Father Michael, and Hannah soon joined us.

I wondered if when I was a fussy baby my father said the words of the Mass in my ear. I always found it settling, soothing.

As we knelt at the rail to receive communion, I could feel Chloe quivering next to me. I looked over and saw the tears running off her nose and chin. Chloe was an agnostic, as I suspect everyone is at eighteen. I was surprised her tears were during Mass, the ceremony she attended only to please me. As we left the rail after communion, she slumped to the floor in a faint. Too much blood to the uterus, not enough to the brain, or was it the heart?

CHAPTER THREE

Father Michael helped me get Chloe upstairs. She hadn't changed from her after-shower sweats so we just slipped her between the covers. Michael excused himself, and I sat on the edge of the bed.

'Feeling better?' I knew she must be. Some color was returning to her face.

'I feel stupid. I thought this only happened in bad movies.' What, fainting or pregnancy?

'I fainted quite a bit with you. If I recall it has something to do with the blood supply going to the uterus and the brain being deprived of oxygen, something like that.' I fainted quite a bit both times, if the truth be told.

'Mother, you have one of the great scientific minds. God, I feel weird. How long does this last?'

'First three months, if memory serves. Just take it easy for a few minutes afterwards. Pretty soon you'll recognize them coming and you'll have a chance to sit down. They only happen when you're standing up, so you don't need to worry about driving. Maybe you'll be lucky and this will only happen once.'

'Lucky isn't the word I would use to describe myself right now. Do you know I can't do anything about this for another four weeks? The doctor said I should take a month to think about it. It's going to be the longest month of my life.' Chloe rolled on her side and pulled the comforter under her chin.

'A month seems like a very short time to make a decision about this. I know we agreed not to discuss this until after the funeral, but it really is very hard to ignore.'

'Yeah. Decisions, decisions. I just wish I didn't have to wait. It would be so much easier to get rid of a little cluster of cells. I hate to think, to know, that it keeps growing. By the time I can get rid of it, the heart is beating and it's even growing little hairs.'

'It certainly sounds like you've done your research.'

'Do you remember that book you gave me when Aunt Susan was pregnant with Lucy? I was about six? It had all those photographs of babies, fetuses in the womb?' How odd Chloe would use a word like 'womb'. Womb, home, milk, love. Four-letter words of comfort.

'I remember. I wanted you to understand that the baby wasn't in her stomach rolling around with the tuna sandwiches. I remember thinking just that when I was a kid.' My parents didn't discuss sex with me until I was ten. My mother sat me down with several diagrams of the human reproductive system and confused the hell out of me. Somehow either she deleted or I missed the information on how the tadpole gets to the egg to start things rolling. Since everything was microscopic I assumed the sperm could wiggle through the warp and woof of clothing to hit paydirt. I didn't slow dance until the eighth grade when Susan filled in the gaps in my education.

'I pulled it out of a box of books in my closet this afternoon. It was right there with my Nancy Drews – let's get rid of those by the way. Anyway, I wanted to reassure myself that this thing would be about the size of a booger when I got rid of it. Well, it will be only about half an inch long, but it's becoming a person, at least a potential person. Maybe I'll get lucky and miscarry. One out of every four pregnancies ends in a miscarriage. Then I wouldn't need to do anything.'

'You can probably forget about a miscarriage. Since you've already had morning sickness and fainting, I think we can assume that your hormones are doing their job.'

'What time is it anyway?' Not original, by any means, but she did manage to change the subject.

'Almost half-past eight. Are you hungry, do you want something to eat?' Mangia, Mangia. Perhaps I had been Italian in a past life.

'No. I think I'd just like to sleep, if you don't mind. But I'll stay up if you want company.'

'I think I'll go to bed after I grab something to eat. When did Susan leave by the way?' I hadn't had a chance to say goodbye.

'Just before Father Studley-Do-Right came to get me for Mass. She said she would be by in the morning but she would call first to see if we need anything. Where is Father Studley from? I would remember seeing him.'

'He's from the Cathedral, I suppose. I just met him today. He seems like a nice enough kid.' I knew I must be getting old – doctors, dentists, and priests were all starting to look young. 'Speaking of Father Studley, who is, in real life, Michael Blaine, I bet he is still here. I'd better go release him to the world. I'll see you in the morning, sweetheart.' I hugged her briefly and turned out the lights as I left the room.

As I suspected, Michael was still taking care of business, manning the now quiet phone and door. Young priests are so dedicated. They are dedicated to their God, their jobs, their women. I'd never known a priest to get into really hot water before thirty.

'Hi, Michael. Keeping the watch fires burning?'

'I wanted to see how your daughter is doing. I thought

you might need me to take her someplace, go to a pharmacy or something.' I couldn't help wondering if he would be so interested if it had been my Great-Aunt Maude with the whiskers on her chin who had fainted.

'She'll be fine. She's probably asleep by now. Thanks for your concern.'

'Does she have diabetes or something?' He hadn't learned yet how to ask rude questions in a polite way.

'No, she is as healthy as they come. Pregnancy isn't considered a disease; it's a condition. A damned inconvenient, perhaps tragic, condition.' I was conditioned to tell priests the whole truth. 'I shouldn't have told you that. Obviously that information isn't for general distribution. Let's keep it off the Bishop's desk if we can.' Odd, but I felt better for the telling. I wasn't quite ready to be a guest on a talk show, but perhaps I could be one of those nice women in the audience who make passionate statements in quivering voices. Susan could come with me and we could have lunch at Tavern on the Green. Of course, that's assuming that I want to say something passionate on *Donahue*. If I really must say something on *Oprah* we would have to go to Chicago, and I loathe Chicago.

'I wouldn't dream of saying anything. Didn't I hear Chloe is some kind of genius child who is getting her degree at eighteen?' Michael had learned how to charm mothers.

'She is an eighteen-year-old college senior, but being bright certainly doesn't stop her from doing stupid things. Maybe it makes things harder. She has been living with kids who are three or four years older for quite a while. I always felt she handled it just fine. Maybe she did.' My stomach had been gnawing at me for a while and I realized I hadn't really had anything all day except beer and sherry. 'Are you hungry? I'm going to raid the kitchen. You are welcome to join me.' I've always loved feeding people, even pot-luck suppers late at night. I used to think it was a reflection of my generous spirit until I realized it was a gracious way to control other people's lives. I spent several thousand dollars and five months talking to a black-haired woman in Greenwich to figure this out. She felt it was a breakthrough, but I gave her a cheese danish at our next and last appointment.

'Thanks, I'd love to get something to eat before I head back.' Men are great to feed at this age. Their bellies are still flat and they haven't developed many taste buds. They will clean their plates as well as any young dog.

'When did everyone else leave?' We walked toward the kitchen.

'Right after Mass. That reminds me, your secretary said the florist is coming at ten in the morning. She said you would be pleased.'

'I am, as a matter of fact. I haven't slept through the night in months, and tomorrow morning I can sleep in till nine if I want. Not only that, but in three or four days I am going to have this place to myself again. I feel as though I've been living in Grand Central Station for weeks.' The house had been filled for weeks with well-meaning people, begging me to let them do things. I had been tempted several times to offer them my hand laundry. One group of crinkly old ladies felt they were a comfort to me because they sat for hours in my living room and drank coffee.

'This place kind of looks like Grand Central. I can't imagine actually living here.'

'It's all what you're used to. I've lived here all my life except for college and when I was married.' I glanced around the old kitchen, trying to see it through the young man's eyes. Although familiar to me, I supposed it could seem imposing, designed, as it was, for big families and even bigger parties.

'Are you divorced?' He just needed to phrase things differently.

'Widowed. Chloe's father died almost seventeen years ago. I came home for a few days and never got around to leaving.' I turned on the lights above the table and opened the refrigerator. 'Things look better in here.' Hannah had cleared out the deli wrappings and the white carry-out cartons. She had also done away with all the little pots filled with God-knows-what that I had been shoving to the back of the shelf for weeks. 'Looks like cold roast beef, fried chicken, some kind of potato thing. What sounds good?'

'Chicken looks good.' The young priest was eyeing the contents of the refrigerator over my shoulder.

'Oh hell, pull it all out. I'll set the table. Grab me a diet soda, please.' I pulled out two plates and noticed again one was chipped. I'd been looking at the same chip for months and had told myself dozens of times I needed to replace dishes. I was surprised that Hannah hadn't mentioned all the neglectful chips and nicks that lurked in the room. She'd probably been too overwhelmed by the furry bits in the pots.

We ate quickly and in silence for several minutes. I often ate alone of late and was comfortable with the silence, but I wasn't sure that he was.

'How long have you been with the Cathedral?'

'I'm not really with the Cathedral, not on the staff. I'm finishing up some post-grad stuff and picking up a little supply priest time when I can. They called me this afternoon and asked me to come over and help out here.'

'Are you one of his priests?' He seemed nice enough but nothing is cast in stone.

'Is this an interview?'

'No, I'm just trying to decide if I like you or not. His Purpleness and I don't see eye to eye on many things. If you are one of his priests, we can avoid discussing all those things we will disagree on. That doesn't leave us a whole lot to talk about outside the weather, but at least we won't be at each other's throats.'

'I gathered there was little love lost between Bishop Mark and your father. To answer your question, I'm not one of the Bishop's men. I'm fairly mainstream. In fact, I don't get many assignments from the Cathedral. I also teach part-time at Holbrook to pay the rent.' Holbrook was a small, liberal arts college outside Derryton.

'Where are you from?'

'Tacoma, Washington. I came back here for school, but I'm pretty sure I'd like to stay. I really love the East. Anything else you'd like to know? Would you like to take notes, get a copy of my curriculum vitae?' He grinned at me. Nice big teeth, a good-looking young man.

'Okay, okay, I'm being nosy.' But he was eating my food and prying into my life. Priests rarely see the flip side.

'I'm just teasing you. Can I ask you about Chloe?' If I'd said 'no', he still would have asked. Priestly privilege. There is no such thing as a humble priest.

'Why?'

'I just wondered if she was getting any counseling? She's awfully young, and I thought she might benefit from the parenting classes that are given through the hospital.'

'Chloe will probably have an abortion.'

'Can't you stop her?'

'I wouldn't stop her if I could. This is her life, not mine. It has to be her decision.' A reaction to growing up liberal in a conservative town, I always spout the liberal line whether I believe it or not.

'What about the child's life? Your grandchild. You could raise it if she doesn't want to, you—'

'Michael, stop right there. You have no idea what you are talking about. No man in the world knows what he is talking about when it comes to birth and abortion. It was a mistake, a tragic mistake, and it's one monumental decision, but it is

Chloe's. Nobody can or should make that choice for her.'

'If you saw a murder being committed, wouldn't you try to stop it? Why isn't an abortion murder?'

'It becomes murder when the child can live independently of the mother's body. We are not talking about a child here, we are talking about something which could become a child. Is an egg a chicken?' I got up and opened the refrigerator. 'Do you want a beer? I've got Spartan dark and Millers.'

'Great, I'd love a dark. Who got her pregnant? Doesn't he have a say in any of this?' He didn't miss a beat between beer and boyfriend. I began to wonder if he might have a true vocation.

'Michael, as a priest, you really need to learn to rephrase some of your questions. I don't mind all that much because I'm fairly rude myself, but it could hurt your career. I can be as rude as I want, but you can't afford that.' I looked at him expectantly.

'Okay, try this; is your daughter involved with an appropriate significant other?' More big teeth. I liked this guy. Good hair, good teeth, and a nice healthy body. His grin showed that he expected to be liked. Somebody had given this boy a lot of food and love.

'Better, needs work, but better.' I sat on the floor in front of the stove to drink my beer. Before I finished the first sip, Russ was in my lap and I noticed Meg eyeing the leftovers on the table. 'As you have probably figured out, I don't run a tight ship. You can feed the dogs scraps if you want.'

'Don't change the subject. You gave me a beer so I know you're not planning to kick me out. Who's the father?' A true priest, he didn't doubt I would tell him.

'A fairly insignificant other. Some frat rat from Colorado, a sperm donor with biceps. Certainly not the love of her life. He doesn't even know about this.'

'Don't you think he should be told? I would want to

know.' He would want to know the day, the hour, and the ph level.

'Michael have you ever gotten a girl pregnant?' I could be as rude as any priest.

'No.'

'Are you sure, absolutely sure?' He was too old, and too beautiful to be a virgin. I was fairly certain that he had put a song in the heart of more than one sweet young choral mistress.

'What are you trying to say?' Old trick of the priest; a question for a question.

'I'm not sure. Maybe I'm just trying to say this is not male territory. You are excluded by biology, but you, you guys, are always trying to control it, to manage it. It doesn't belong to you or any other man. You should all stay out of what you can't understand.'

'But men are a part of it. You want us to support our children, provide for our families.'

'Yes, if we choose to have children. But before that, before they become children, they belong to the woman. The whole process has been taken away from us. We aren't chattels; we aren't incubators.'

'Of course you're not chattels or incubators. Nobody says you are. But you can't expect men to step out of the whole process. Men have a right to children, just as women do.' He was neglecting his food. Perhaps he was squeamish. Sex and abortion can put some off their feed.

'Having children isn't a right, it's a responsibility. The biggest one in the world. Men want to control the process because they can't have women control the most important thing in the world. Western civilization is based on men controlling other men, women, nature. What if he has to come to grips with the fact women control what is most important? Why do you think rape is on the rise, domestic violence, sexual abuse? Because man is scared.'

'Who is man? All men aren't ogres. Most men are nice guys who just want to get by and be left alone.' He leaned forward, intense and so young.

'Man is society, the Church, the patriarchy, the government, which tells women from the time they are girls they are valued for their fecundity, at least the suggestion of fecundity. "He" tells us we have to be young, beautiful, have breasts that would be the envy of a nursing mother of triplets.'

'Don't you think you're overstating all this? You're painting everything with an awfully broad brush.'

'What I think is I've made you think. I think you will wake up tomorrow wishing you had known what to say to me tonight.' I knew I would be thinking of things I wish I had said.

'The Bishop told me you might present certain challenges.'

'I bet he did. He was wrong, of course. I can be a really lovely person, but I have chosen not to share that with him. However, as a one-time special death event, I promise you will see me as a lovely person for the next three days. On one condition, of course.'

'One condition?'

'Stay away from my daughter.' You and everyone who looks like you.

'I can arrange for another priest to come over tomorrow. I don't want to make you uncomfortable.' He sounded hurt and surprised. He was no doubt used to middle-aged women fawning over him while they pretended a maternal concern. He was too green on one hand, too old on the other.

'Actually, you make me quite comfortable. Also, you need the money, and if the Bishop wants to pay to have my door answered, I'd like it to be you opening the door. Typical of His Purpleness, he didn't ask if I wanted or needed anyone, but I must admit it has been nice not to worry about the door or phone.' Not a bad deal really, the Bishop paying for a butler. I wondered if he could send over a masseuse?

'I will stay away from Chloe, but if she asks for my counsel I will jump in and tell her what I think.'

'Chloe is not a believer, not right now, anyway. I expect her to come back to Mother Church at some time. I did. I can't imagine her going to you or any other priest for advice. Don't forget, she grew up in a bishop's home. Priests don't impress her.' I liked the way the words tasted in my mouth. I liked describing the independence of my daughter, which I didn't share.

'I take it they don't impress you a great deal either?'

'Some do, some don't. I would like to remind you the Church's stand on abortion is one of choice. The Roman Catholics have enough blackbirds harassing abortion clinics without needing help from the Episcopalians.'

'Do you really care what the Church teaches on abortion?' Did I really care what the Church taught on anything?

'I'm always interested in what the Church teaches, but like all good Episcopalians, I make up my own mind. If I didn't want to think for myself I would be a Roman or a Baptist.' I sounded like a bright, rebellious teenager.

'Why didn't you ever remarry? You seem very angry with men.' The rudest question yet. Apparently he had been reading some pop-psychology articles in the Sunday supplements.

'Such clichés! Sometimes I'm angry with men, sometimes I'm angry with women, sometimes I'm angry at people in general. That, dear Michael, is the human condition. I don't hate men, and I don't think my marital status has anything to do with this conversation. You disappoint me. What was your term, "using a broad brush"? You are using a broad brush to paint me as an angry manhater because I don't agree with you and don't want to be "counseled" by you. You can do better than that.' How did the Church expect to exist into the next century if this was what they were turning out?

'I apologize if I offended you. I should head back to my place, it's getting late.' He rose and put his dish in the sink. 'You're sure you want me back in the morning?'

'Absolutely. I don't think you need to worry about getting here much before nine.'

'That's fine. I'll see myself out and lock the front door as I leave. I've already checked the other doors.' He got up to leave. 'Good night. I enjoyed dinner and our talk.'

'Good night, Michael. And, Michael, I meant what I said, stay away from my daughter.' I smiled and he nodded back, pulling an imaginary lock of hair down his forehead.

I filled the bathtub with the hottest water I could stand. It had been weeks since I could enjoy a late night bath, and I wanted this one to last a long time. I soaked, shaved my legs, took a pumice stone to my feet, all the time-consuming things. I could understand why a cat purrs while it licks its fur.

Ruddy and warm, I pulled on an old flannel gown and a fluffy robe. I reached for the phone and dialed and leaned back on my bed, looking forward to hearing his voice.

'Hello.' Warm as my fluffy robe.

'Hi, Elliott. How are things in the land of the reasonably sane?'

'How are you Jill? I called Mary, and she said to come over. I called a second time and some guy said you weren't seeing anyone.'

'Wires got crossed, I guess. I would have seen you.' I pictured him in his paisley robe, long legs stretched in front of the fire. After years of celibacy, I was shocked at what fun an 'escort' could be.

'Mary filled me in. Are you all right? I could come over.'

'I'm fine, at least about Dad. Isn't Ben already in bed?' His twelve-year-old son is my godson; his late wife was one of my best friends. We had known each other so well and so long at first I felt I was screwing my brother. Kip Borden had wounded me, but Rick and his death had all but finished me off. I'd never have gotten involved with Elliott if I hadn't been so damned tired from taking care of Dad. My defenses were down and I still can't recall how we ended up in bed one warm October afternoon. The sun was setting before I remembered my determination to let my vagina atrophy from lack of use.

'He's in bed, but Theta is here.' Theta was about the fifth or sixth housekeeper Elliott had hired in the last two years. 'I could come over for a while, or even longer.' I heard the smile in his voice. Because of Ben and my father, our couplings had been confined to what used to be referred to as nooners. I wasn't in a terrible rush to have him see me before a morning shower, to smell his morning mouth, or listen to his nocturnal flatulence. After seventeen years, I had grown used to my virgin couch.

'I'm going to pass on more guests, not that you're a guest exactly. I've had a hell of a day and just climbed out of the bath. I'm ready for bed.'

'Are you naked?' My own obscene caller.

'I'm wearing a flannel nightgown, but I did shave my legs.' I'd neglected things like that lately.

'If I can't come over, I would rather not talk about your legs or what's between them.' He was sweet, knowing I hated my short legs and chubby thighs. 'How's Chloe? Mary said she got in in time.'

'Chloe came in bearing bombshells. She's pregnant and planning to have an abortion.' I swallowed hard. I felt as though the pregnancy was carried in my throat, instead of Chloe's womb.

'Oh, Jill. Are you sure you don't want me to come over?'

'You're sweet, Elliott, but I'm really all right. I'm looking forward to having my first quiet night in months.' I fluffed the pillows against my headboard.

'I can be quiet.'

'No you can't.' I giggled, Chloe and my father forgotten. Elliott made wonderful noises when we were in bed.

'I could try to be quiet.'

'Another time. I do appreciate the groveling, I must admit.' I coiled the telephone cord around my index finger. A thirteen-year-old again.

'Well, love, sleep well. I'll stop by first thing in the morning.' Love was a term of endearment, not a declaration. Elliott would always love Sally. He felt he had given his best, but whatever was left was given freely. I usually didn't mind because I knew how demanding the dead can be.

'I'm sleeping in tomorrow. Stop by for lunch if you can.'

'Will do. Good night, Jill.'

'Night, Elliott.'

The house didn't have ghosts. Believe me, I'd looked. When I was eleven or twelve I read everything I could about ghosts and hauntings. Susan shared my interest in things that go bump in the night. Since the palace looked somewhat like a very well-maintained haunted house, we felt sure all the residents weren't accounted for. We set up cameras, stayed up late, played with an ouija board, everything we could think of, including the performance of a few ceremonies we felt anyone in the spectral plane would find enticing. Nothing.

I came to the conclusion then, and nothing afterwards changed my mind, that those walls couldn't support ghosts. The Wolden who built this house probably poured something into the foundation that makes the house toxic to them. Ghosts suggest lack of fulfillment and unfinished business. Woldens don't stare out the window dreaming of what might have been. Woldens straighten their spines, lift their chins, and go do something useful. We do good works and challenge others to do the same, We finish our business, at least most of us do.

I went into his room. I'd watched him die, held his hand, but I was still surprised he wasn't there. The carpet held the marks of that awful bed, and the space gaped before me. I supposed that for months I would be listening for him, looking for him. I've read that it's common to see the deceased for months after a death, but I saw nothing that night.

'Good night.' My voice sounded huge in my ears. I wanted, needed, to say more, but the roar of my voice made me mute, vibrating in my head, as I walked back to my room, holding my hand against the wall for balance.

I awoke to the unmistakable sounds of hounds in the hallway. Russell was whining to come in, and Chloe was trying to keep him quiet, without success.

'Mom, are you awake?' I thought about ignoring her, playing possum.

'I am now. Come on in everybody.' The door banged open as the dogs jockeyed into position for the spot closest to my hand. Chloe followed with a breakfast tray. She was wearing baggy shorts, an oversize tee-shirt with Greek lettering (his shirt?) and running shoes. Her hair was piled on top of her head, and she looked like a cross-dressing Gibson Girl.

'Sorry to wake you, Mom, but it's almost nine. The florist is coming at ten and Aunt Susan will be here at half-past ten. She said something about shopping. I was only half listening.'

'Are you going running? Do you think that's wise?'

'I'm fine. I don't feel dizzy, and it's going to be a gorgeous day. I brought you some coffee, and Father Studley brought some pastries. Isn't this weird looking?' She showed me a circular pastry with a peach half, round side up in the middle. 'This is your brain on drugs.'

'You're full of yourself this morning. Your father was always full of piss and vinegar in the morning. Thank God, I am at least on a more civilized internal clock.' I eased into the morning and began to respond to stimuli around the third cup of coffee. I could force communication before the first, but it was a huge effort. I pointedly stared at Chloe's outfit. 'I really think you should forgo running for a few days.'

'I knew you would say that, so I've already finished my run.' She grinned and lifted her arm to show the wet half-moon on her shirt.

'You're a brat. Thanks for the coffee. Anybody here yet?' I took a gulp of the coffee and imagined the cheering molecules of caffeine invading my blood.

'Father Studley, of course. He said Mary called. She won't be here until ten. Hannah is due in at eleven, and she is going to put out a cold buffet for lunch. Jenny is downstairs with two other cleaning ladies. She said she wants to do upstairs before four this afternoon. And last but not least, I'm picking up Grandma at the airport at three.'

'Just Grandma?' Eleanor had remarried after the death of Rick's father. Her new husband, Les Holmes, was a retired orthopedist. My step-father-in-law?

'Just Grandma. Les couldn't come, she didn't say why.' I had been counting on Les to give Eleanor someone to fuss at other than me.

'It sounds like things are popping. Have you been working out? You really look buffed.' She reminded me of Rick, all long bone and lean muscle.

'Buff, Mom, the word is buff. I've been working out with weights this semester. Speaking of buff, do you suppose Father Studley became a priest because he knows how beautiful he looks in black with a touch of white?'

'Have you talked to him?'

'Mostly looked. He seems nice enough.' She'd been flirting, that's why she was so cheerful.

'I had dinner with him last night. He's a hard line pro-lifer. I told him to stay away from you. Let me know if he bothers you.'

'You told him I was pregnant?' She looked away.

'He stayed around to see how you were. It was very nice really. He thought we might need his help to take you some place. He assumed you were an epileptic or a diabetic. I know I shouldn't have said anything, but he caught me at a weak moment.' I couldn't quite remember what a strong moment felt like.

'At least he won't say anything, I suppose. Funny isn't it, I didn't care if anybody knew I was sleeping with Will, but I don't want anyone to know about this. I'm really ashamed. I feel like I've got a scarlet A on my forehead.'

'You don't have anything on your forehead. I was just thinking that you've never looked more beautiful.' Actually I had been wondering how she would look with a big belly. I wondered if a pregnancy would stretch her boyish hips, or if she would have one of those neat 'basketball' pregnancies.

'You sound like my mother. I wonder what Grandpa would have said, about my being pregnant.' The enthusiasm of a moment ago was gone. She laid down next to me and stuffed a pillow under her head.

'Your grandfather adored you, but he was pretty rigid in many ways. Does it really matter what he would have thought?' I knew it did. My father had the moral authority of God. I knew what God looked like.

'It matters. He and Grandy would have been appalled. I'm sorry, I said we wouldn't talk about this until after the funeral, but I can't think of anything else. Sometimes everything seems completely normal, then I remember. I feel like I've been invaded.'

'That's pretty accurate if you think about it. One alien cell, and your whole body starts changing.' Her whole body, her whole future. Her girlhood invaded and destroyed.

'Do you think I'd be doing the right thing, getting an abortion?' She rolled onto her back.

'I can't answer that, Chloe. I'd love to answer it. I'd love to take this over and manage the whole thing, but I can't do that. This is your life, your body, your future, and your baby. Nobody, nobody, can make this decision for you. I hate the thought of you having an abortion, but I sure as hell don't think anybody, including me, has a right to tell you, or any other woman, that she has to reproduce.'

'That's probably the very worst thing you could say to me right now.'

'I'm sorry, I really am. What's the very best thing I could say?'

'Exactly what you said. That I have to do this, that I can do it: I usually feel so competent and in charge, but right now I feel like I'm about ten. I feel like I can't even be trusted to comb my hair. I want you to take care of me. I don't want to decide.' Chloe was crying, tears falling past her ears, soaking into her hair.

I sat further up in bed and pulled her toward me. I rocked her back and forth and hummed softly to her as I had done when she was tiny. Rocked back and forth as we have since long before we left the trees. The rhythm of mothers, given to us the first time we hold our child. I could almost feel the golden cord, tying us together, leading back to the trees, traveling forward to Chloe's child. I rocked them both, I rocked us all.

CHAPTER FOUR

'I want profusion, a woodland feel. I don't want anything formal – no gladioli.' The florist had brought sample flowers and design books for my approval. He kept spreading out pictures featuring horrible, geometric arrangements with pointy, hot-house blooms and tropical grasses.

'I thought you would want something more classic, if you will. After all, the service will be at the Cathedral and he was the Bishop for all those years.' He was becoming slightly exasperated with me. Billy Simpson had been running the largest floral business in town for the last two decades. He had been 'out' before it was fashionable and considered himself the arbiter of taste and beauty for the surrounding area. Actually, Billy did know my taste, and I suspected he had already decided I would handle the service like a state occasion. Clever businessman that he was, he had probably been placing orders for the flowers he thought I would order and was wondering if it was too late to cancel the orders. Billy loved to do the silly limp-wrist bit around giggling matrons, but I suspected he was one of the sharpest businessmen in town. In addition to the florist shop, he owned two hair salons, an apartment building, and a fast-food franchise.

'Well, way back when, long before he was a bishop, he was a farmboy. He loved informal gardens, wildflowers, vines, and meadows. That's the look I want, Billy. And I want those arrangements you did for the Guild benefit, different colors of course, at the luncheon.'

'Whatever you say, Mrs Parkhurst.' Billy usually called me Jill. 'I'll do the best I can, but don't forget Easter is one day after the service. I can't guarantee a big variety of flowers.' Billy tended to whine, but his martyrdom hadn't hurt his business.

'I'm sure everything will be wonderful, Billy, it always is.' I was fairly certain that Billy had already figured the bill to within three dollars.

'Do you want to know what all this is going to cost?'

'No. I want to enjoy it. Just send the bill. I have to go check on a few things, but feel free to call and talk to Mary if you have any questions.'

'Thank you. Have a nice day, Mrs Parkhurst.' His voice was just this side of sarcastic.

'You're very welcome, Billy.' Mine was sarcastic.

I left the room, and Billy headed into the dining room to measure for arrangements. Billy had been our florist for at least fifteen years, and I was annoyed he hadn't offered any sympathy, any words of comfort. This was just another order, another job. I wanted everyone to mourn my loss, honor my bereavement. Of course, I also wanted to be declared the official center of the universe, and that hadn't happened yet either. Life goes on.

Mary had made menu selections for the luncheon, which I approved. She delivered a fresh stack of messages and had marked those she felt merited my immediate attention. Depressingly few things actually needed my attention. Time on my hands, hours to fill, seemed very strange.

*

Susan and Father Michael were laughing in the front hall. Men of all ages loved Susan. Baby boys to old men always smiled more when she was in the room. I had watched many a gut sucked in when Susan was around. She was tall, slim, a silvery blonde, but it was much more than that. Men liked to get close enough to sniff the air around her, share her magnetic field. Five hundred years ago they would have had her dance naked in the fields to insure the crops and their own erections. They would have saved her milk and used it in potions, fought each other for a lock of pubic hair, a holy relic. From the sounds in the hall, Michael had fallen under her spell.

'Morning everyone.' Susan hugged me, and I smiled at Michael, knowing he would love to be hugged by Susan. 'How are you, Jilly? You look great, rested.' Susan was patting my hair into place, brushing lint from my shoulder.

'I feel good. I can't remember the last time I slept through the night. Mary has everything under control, and I've pissed off the florist, but that's another story.'

'Oh, Billy is always pissed off. Do you have a black dress for tomorrow? I thought maybe we could find something if you didn't.' Susan knows where to buy anything in the tri-state area.

'I still have that black Chanel suit I bought ten years ago. By some miracle, it still fits.' Yankee to the bone, use it up, wear it out. It was awfully tight across the waist and bust but I could hold it in for a few hours. I led Susan toward the stairs, nodded to Michael.

'Jill, a minute please.' Father Michael wasn't going to let me leave yet. I supposed he was going to tell me what he had decided he should have told me last night.

'Yes, Michael?'

'Good Friday services begin at noon today. I'll be happy to take you if you don't feel like driving.' A gentle reminder

I should be keeping my mind on the spiritual today. Enough of clothes and flowers.

'Thanks for reminding me, Michael. You go ahead without me. I've just spent three months observing Good Friday. I'm holding out for Easter.'

I wanted to annoy, but clearly I had amused him. He smiled, touched his finger to his tongue and drew a line on an imaginary blackboard. One point for me. 'We will all miss you, Jill.'

When we were out of earshot, Susan turned to me. 'What was all that about?'

'We kind of got into it last night. Chloe passed out in the chapel and Michael helped me get her into bed. He was concerned, and I explained she was pregnant, that she didn't have some movie-of-the-week disease. We got off on the whole life versus choice, man versus woman thing. God save us from twenty-five-year-olds who know everything. Bottom line is, I told him to stay away from Chloe. She doesn't need her own personal Operation Rescue.'

'Is she all right this morning?'

'She was fine when she woke up. She went for a run, looked wonderful. Of course after two minutes of talking about it, she was in tears. Poor kid. The situation is bad enough, but she's got enough hormones pumping through her to turn Sly Stallone into Bernadette Peters.'

'Let's go find her and have a hormone talk before she thinks she's lost her mind.' Susan is something of an expert on the emotional effects of pregnancy. 'By the way, I want you and Chloe at the house on Easter. I knew you wouldn't have the time, or the inclination, so I've made a basket for Chloe. I've already told the children you are coming, so say yes.'

'Yes. Yes, and thank you.' Holidays at Susan's house are enough to make you feel sorry for Martha Stewart's guests because they're not all at Susan's.

'Where is Chloe?'

'She was on my bed the last time I saw her. We should check there first.'

Chloe was still on my bed, asleep, curled in the fetal position. Her pillow was wet, crushed under her cheek. I remembered a girl in my dorm. She had always been sleeping and left in the middle of the semester because of mono. Had 'mono' been a code word for pregnancy that I had been too ignorant to know about? Was I sent to England because of 'mono'?

'Chloe, wake up, baby. Susan is here, and we want to talk to you.'

'I fell asleep. Just a minute, I need to pee.' Chloe pulled herself off the bed and shook her head as she walked to my bathroom. Susan and I sat down on the sofas near the fireplace. As the moments passed, we heard the sounds of retching in the next room. Retching, flushing, water running.

'They shoot horses don't they?' Chloe came out of the bathroom looking white and damp. She lay down on the sofa and put her head in my lap. Her skin felt cold as I stroked her cheek. 'How long does this last? I feel like hell.'

'Usually the first three months. Sometimes dry crackers help. I'll bring over some blackberry tea later. Some women swear by it.' Susan had tried all the remedies at least six times. She loved the role of wise woman, midwife to the masses. She loved to chat up pregnant women in stores, judge their bellies, approve their progress.

'I wish this were over. I'm not sure I can take four more weeks of this.'

'Do you mean the nausea?' I suspected she didn't.

'Being pregnant. When I was running this morning, I felt so good I started thinking I could even have the baby, but I know I can't. I know I don't want to have it. I can't do anything I need to do if I have a baby. I've worked too hard to get into this program. I'm not kissing it goodbye. I don't even know if I ever want to have children. I can't think clearly right now.' The first time Chloe went to summer camp I lost her to khaki shorts and tents. She loved eating cold food outside, sleeping on rocks, peeing behind bushes. A graduate program in a Mexican slum sounded like Nirvana to her. Getting a degree for camping out under the worst possible circumstances. Such a deal. Twenty-six thousand dollars a year so that my daughter could flirt with dysentery and cholera.

'Trust me, Chloe, a lot of what you are feeling is due to the hormones. Mood swings are very common at this stage of a pregnancy. Mood swings and exhaustion. This is very normal. I didn't even know I was pregnant the third time until I found myself sobbing in the A & P because they didn't have fresh clams. What you're feeling is very normal, trust me.' Susan was not going to give up her wise woman routine.

'Chloe, if you decide to keep this baby, you won't be alone. A lot of wonderful people have been raised by single mothers, yourself included. I could certainly adjust to being a grandmother, and God knows we have the room for a crib.' I didn't want to push her, but I could almost feel the baby in my arms.

'I can't palm a baby off on you like a stray kitten. I have nothing to give a kid. I wish I didn't have to go back for finals. I would like to stay here for the next month and sleep. I'd like to wake up in a pool of blood and know it's over. I wish I could just take a pill. I know I could swallow a pill, I just don't know if I can put my feet in stirrups in some clinic.'

'There are always options, Chloe. If you don't want the baby, someone else will.' Susan idly brushed at lint on her dark skirt as she suggested the option.

'Do you mean adoption?' She said the word as though she wasn't sure how it was pronounced.

'No, don't consider that, please. I couldn't bear for you to go through that. I couldn't stand to have my grandchild go to strangers.' I felt sweat between my breasts. I looked at Susan, willing her to make eye contact with me. She did, and I shook my head slightly. I couldn't talk about this anymore or I would start vomiting myself.

'Honey, I just want you to know I love you like one of my own. If I can help?' Susan shrugged her shoulders and straightened her skirt. Her speciality was pregnancy, not its termination.

'Thank you, Aunt Susie, that means a lot, really. I know you both love me and want to help, but neither of you can begin to understand what I'm going through. I can't even begin to describe what this is like, I don't expect you to understand.'

'Chloe, I understand more than you think.' Here goes.

'No you don't! I'm sorry, but you don't. I know how it was for both of you. A happy husband who wanted you to sit down, and loved to put his ear to your pink tummy. Maternity smocks with lace collars, buying layettes in the city after a light lunch at the Russian Tea Room. Forgive me if I'm not quite as romantic as you two!' Her voice was a low growl of anger. 'I'm going to shower and get ready to pick up Grandma at the airport.' Chloe was at the door.

'Chloe, come sit down. I need to talk to you.'

'No, no more of this. I can't even think about this anymore.' She was gone.

Susan looked at me blandly. 'Coward.'

'I tried, sort of. If I knew it would help, I would tell her. I'm not at all sure it would make a difference. Eighteen-year-olds don't listen to their mothers, it's the law. Airing my dirty laundry is not going to change anything.'

'You don't know that, Jill. It's certainly what you want to

believe, but that doesn't make it the truth. Maybe it isn't what you believe at all. Why did you start to tell her if you didn't think it would make any difference?'

'I wanted to make a connection. No, that's not it, not really. I guess I was hoping she would let me have the baby. I can't help but think of it as a baby, I know I shouldn't. It's just going to be that much worse when she gets rid of it. I look ahead and I just don't see much. I'm going to be a little old lady, living alone in an old house. God, how I envy you and your brood.'

'So you think the baby will come in on a white charger? Babies grow up, Jill. You *are* going to be an old lady in this house unless you die or sell the house, and move with a life of your own.'

'I do have a life of my own. It is not your life but it is my life and I chose it and I am happy with it.' Susan was not above implying that her life of husband and numerous children was preferable to mine. 'I think maybe it has something to do with preservation of the species. Maybe all those right to life types are out there because of some biological imperative. Maybe it's all ego. Every pregnant woman has a right to choose unless the fetus carries some of my genetic information. Does that make me a horrible person?' I leaned toward Susan. 'I know I'm going to be a little old lady living in this house, but I want to know that I've got grandchildren somewhere. I want pictures on the kitchen wall that they drew for me. I want to see Rick's eyes on some little kid's face. I want to know that some child can whistle like my father could. I want some child to have my mother's fashion sense. I want to know that a part of me, a part of my family lives on.' I leaned back, watching her face. 'Does that make me a selfish monster?'

'Of course you're not a monster; selfish, but not a monster. Actually, I think you're doing a gang-busters' job of this. You've always been a great mother. Chloe knows that.

You both need some time away from this.' We needed to be years away from it. 'Cheer up, Eleanor will be here in a matter of hours and everything will be right with the world.' As my best friend, Susan can't abide Eleanor.

'I just hope Chloe doesn't decide to unburden herself on Eleanor. Eleanor would just love to gnaw on my leg over that for a while.' I always felt Eleanor was waiting to strip my bones of their flesh, grinning, waiting, her bloody fangs exposed, hoping I would show my soft belly.

'When is she leaving? Do I need to invite her for Easter?' Susan put her hands to her throat in mock strangulation.

'I never thought to ask. I'm hoping she will have to leave right away so Les gets his minimum daily requirement of nagging. I would think she would want to spend Easter with Allison and her family. At least I hope that is the plan.' Allison is my sister-in-law, Rick's older sister. She has three married children and several grandchildren. 'I'm hoping that Allison's will seem more attractive to the old bat.'

'Well, if she's around, bring her along. Kent has a new haircut, so she can complain about that all day.' Kent is Susan's oldest son, a student at William & Mary.

'You are a dear. Not everyone would want Eleanor on a major holiday.' I couldn't think of anyone who would want her on Arbor Day.

'You'd do the same for me. Besides, I have some emotional distance from her. She doesn't make me crazy, at least not immediately.'

'I'm being very unfair to you, Susan. You've got kids, things to do. You really don't need to hang around here. I'm fine, and everything seems under control.' Well, almost everything.

'If you're really sure?' Knowing her so well, I could see that she was pleased to be released.

'I'm sure. Strange, but I've hardly thought about Dad at

all today. I think I'll be a basket case at the service tomorrow, but right now I'm fine.'

'Before I leave, could we look at the hats?'

'What a great idea. Where was my head? Let's go take a look.'

My mother was never concerned about current fashions. Her clothes were simple, well-cut, conservative, usually in neutral colors. She wore the same styles for years without giving a thought to decrees from Seventh Avenue. Her skirts were always one inch below her knees, and she never left the house in trousers, as she called them. She wore powder, lipstick and pulled her long chestnut hair into a chignon at the base of her skull. She never would have admitted to vanity, although she watched her weight religiously. Pretty, in a quiet way, she would have faded into her surroundings had it not been for her hats.

Mother always maintained that her hats were a necessity because of her position as the Bishop's wife and because of her fair skin. She felt people needed to be reminded to dress properly in and out of church and felt that hats set a certain tone, as well as keeping her skin free of freckles. She had sixty-seven hats when she died, I counted and kept them. Some were simple and dignified and some would have made Carmen Miranda green with envy. Each hat rested in black tissue within its own hatbox. Each box was labeled with an extensive description of the hat and when and where she had worn it. My mother was not, by nature, a keeper, a saver. When she died, I didn't find bundles of letters, diaries, or journals. The jewelry she left was the very same, for the most part, that she had inherited. She didn't leave anything of interest in her pockets or purses, but I could have written my mother's biography from her hatboxes.

A week after she died I packed all of her clothes, shoes,

and handbags into boxes to be taken to the Junior League thrift shop. My father would have preferred they go to some charity sponsored by the Church, but Mother was really no more interested in the Church than most company wives are interested in their husbands' office. After the boxes were gone, Susan and I tried on every hat and I began to understand my mother's passion for them. Each was a beautiful example of the milliner's dying art, but also a tiny roof, giving you warmth and privacy, hiding part of you, protecting you from that which you chose not to see.

Susan and I went through the hats every few months. We brushed each other's hair, pinned it up to resemble my mother's. Grooming each other like monkeys, we usually decided not to wear them after all. They would go back into the tissue, and we'd sigh about fashion today and how we missed elegance.

That day was the exception because Easter was coming. Somehow, during the last few years, it had become the rule that we had to wear a hat on Easter Sunday, and it had to be from Mother's collection. Susan and I shared several rules between us though neither of us was sure how they came about.

'The bed's back. I wonder who did that?' My parents' bedroom was restored. Someone had even made up the old four-poster and turned down the covers. I almost expected my mother to walk in and toss her purse on the bed.

'George and the boy priest. I heard them talking about it when I arrived. Hannah insisted that it be done this morning. George was semi-grumbling about it.'

'I'm glad she insisted. I loathe "design by dying". Queen Anne it isn't.'

'Actually, this room could use a little something. Why don't you rip everything out and turn it into a passion pit for you and Elliott? Keep the carpet, but get rid of all the beige. Hang great fabrics around the bed, the sort of things you can wrap around your bodies in the throes of passion. He'd love it.' Susan surveyed the room, no doubt seeing my lumpy self traipsing through yards of damask.

'That's really not such an awful idea. Not the passion pit, but making a few changes around here. This room has always looked the same.' Beige satin had been glamorous in my mother's youth, and freshened through the years it still reigned supreme in the room.

'What about Elliott, while we are on the subject?' Susan cocked her head at me.

'We are not on the subject of Elliott. We were and are discussing making some changes to this room.' I was surprised to see myself glancing at the clock, anxious to see him at lunch.

'Changes to the room could involve moving in a lovely man who is obviously crazy about you.'

'A lovely man who is still in love with his first wife and has a twelve-year-old son who has been through enough already. Elliott and I are friends, and I enjoy being around him. We have lots of time.'

'You and I are friends. Elliott and I are friends. You and Elliott are lovers. Do I need to graph this out for you?' Long married, she adored romance.

'We are lovers, fuckers, fornicators, sodomites. Does that cover it? Are you happy? He's built like a donkey, and sometimes I come before he even touches me. Is that what you needed to hear?' It was all true, but I tried to sound as though I'd made it all up.

'Before he even touches you, really?' Susan squealed like a seventeen-year-old.

'Susan, we haven't even discussed anything long range. Right now we're just enjoying what we've got. I'm not even sure that we could be considered a couple at this point.'

'Well, I consider you a couple, and I think you're great

together.' She started playing with her hair and watching herself in the mirror. Apparently she'd had her say about middle-aged lust in the dust.

I patted the back of the dressing-table chair. 'Sit down, let's do you first.' Susan sat down at the dressing table and I started pinning her hair up. 'What are you wearing for Easter?'

'That white Victorian thing. Remember, I wore it a lot last summer?'

'I love that on you. It makes you look like the last Czarina.' The 'Victorian thing' was a beautiful white voile dress that swept almost to the ground. The bodice was covered with tiny pleats and spidery white embroidery.

'Last Czarina? It makes me look Russian?' She turned and looked at me in surprise.

'Read a book, Susan. The Czars weren't Russian. They were from that same genetic soup that all the royals are from. Actually what that dress reminds me of is what everyone hoped their great-grandmother looked like, especially when you have all your ducklings around you.' The good mother, mother earth, the Blessed Virgin.

'Can you find that one with the lilies and the huge veil? At least I think it had lilies.' Susan usually didn't acknowledge compliments or comments about her appearance. I never knew if she didn't trust the words or didn't hear them because they were said so often. I always savored every compliment and tasted it over and over. I could ride on a compliment about my nice skin for two months.

'This might be it. Is this the one? You've never worn it before.' Out of the tissue came a cloud, a sugary confection.

'That's wonderful, put it on, just above the bun.' I positioned the hat, and she adjusted the veil. Susan was suddenly twenty years old, my daughter's contemporary. 'The biggest mistake we ever made was giving up veils. This is wonderful. Any of those veils long enough to cover my ass and thighs?' She cocked her head and admired her reflection knowing damned well her ass and thighs were still pretty good.

'If I had one, don't you think I would be wearing it?' We'd been complaining about our bodies since we were skinny little girls. We complained when we were teenagers. We were so busy worrying about our bodies when we were young I think we ended up with the sags and softness we feared. The power of visualization. I try not to think about moles with hair growing out of them, dark moons where teeth used to be.

'Are you wearing a hat tomorrow?' Susan fussed with the veil. Tomorrow, another fashion choice. Tomorrow, the official end of my father's time on earth. Eulogized, bid goodbye, confined to photo albums.

'I think I should. I'm going to cry, and I'd love to have something over my face. Do you think it would look too Kennedyesque, too Jackie at the casket?' I didn't want to look like Hollywood's version of the mourning daughter.

'Your mother set a precedent. Wear a hat.' Susan got up and started reading the labels on hatboxes. 'This looks promising, let's take a look.'

I sat at the dressing table, and Susan set a black felt hat with a rolled brim on my head. I pulled down the small strip of veil, leaving only my lips and chin exposed. I looked into my mother's face. 'Do you see that? I've become her. When did this happen? Damn, life is short, I was sixteen last week.'

'I know what you mean.' Susan removed her hat and carefully placed it in its box. 'It scares me sometimes, the way things seem to be speeding up. Two of my children are adults, almost at least. My last baby can read, and I'm getting brown spots on my hands.' She held up her long white hands as proof. I couldn't see any spots.

'Part of this seems great. I don't mind getting older; I like it, I feel powerful, that whole crone thing, I suppose. What gets to me is being the next in line, not being anybody's child. I think there must be a how-to manual that somebody forgot to give me. There are too many gaps in my education. I should be wise by now. I keep thinking there are things I should know, things I should be told. Is the secret of life that nobody knows what to do next? Maybe that's the secret of the Masons, nobody knows jack shit.'

'Remember when the secret to life was the right man and a two-carat engagement ring?' Susan spread herself across my parents' bed like a cat.

'You at least got that right.' I'd always envied Susan her domestic life.

'Right now, Fletch is in such a funk I'm just glad you're getting laid, because I'm sure not. I've just about forgotten what sex is myself.'

'What's Fletch's problem?' Fletcher was the man Ralph Lipshitz wanted to be before he became Ralph Lauren. He was my idea of an almost perfect husband. Having lived without a husband for so many years, I realized my perfect husband would have to have his own bedroom. He would be available for sex whenever I was interested but would always understand when I wasn't. He would have perfect teeth and nails. His belly would be washboard flat, and he would think my thighs were cute. He would always smell of bay rum and never break wind. Right.

'Some crap about "is this all there is?" I think he's annoyed he hasn't been declared God. We all tiptoe around him to maintain the peace, and he's "asleep" every night before I come to bed. Ironic, isn't it? I make your young priest cream his pants, but my dearly beloved won't touch me. What an asshole.'

'I'm sorry.' And I was. Another illusion shattered.

'Don't be. I'm exaggerating, of course. He is a fine man, and I do love him. But he is a terrible pain in the ass. It seems that every seven years we recreate our marriage, make adjustments, change the rules, go seven years and start over. Call it number 478 in the ongoing series of stuff nobody tells you.'

'Nobody knows jack shit.'

'Apparently not. Are we going to find you an Easter hat or not?'

CHAPTER FIVE

We found an Easter hat for me in lavender, the first step up from black in the mourning color chart.

Susan left, and I wandered down to the dining room for lunch. As promised, Hannah had laid out a cold buffet. I was surprised at the number of people in the room, mostly friends of my parents who had stopped by to pay their respects.

My parents' generation seemed to have a measured, almost gracious response to death. I envied their knowledge of the process, some funereal sense that told them whether a visit or a note would be most appreciated. Not the generation that releases balloons at the graveside or has someone with a mail order divinity degree read from Khalil Gibran. Not the generation that urged you to get on with life in three days. They allowed you to pull into the gray air in your head, to honor your grief.

My mother's college roommate, my father's best man, others, gathered to comfort their loved one's child, ladling out generous servings of time and compassion.

'I've thought of you so much, darling. How was he?' Clara questioned me, not out of curiosity, but from the knowledge that I needed to talk, needed to relate my story of death as much as a new mother needs to relate her story of birth. I had no idea how old Clara was. She had seemed old all my life. She lived across the street and had let me play her piano without washing my hands.

'It was almost beautiful. He just slid away. I felt privileged to share it. Does that sound strange?' I thought about crying, and knew tears were allowed. Allowed, they went unshed.

'That's the way it should be, just slipping away. We don't look at it that way anymore because it doesn't sell movies and books, but that's the way it is. It is an ordinary thing, a natural thing.'

'Chloe was there, too. I'm glad she made it in time.' I took Clara's hand and ran my thumb over the twisted cords, the papery skin.

'Your hands feel like ice, Jill. Give me the other one, and I'll rub them warm.' Is that something else my generation has lost, the soothing touch, hands that heal? 'Death is a good thing for a young person to see. I don't mean some awful, bloody thing, but a nice death. An old, sick person like dear, dear James, just slipping away.'

'I can't think of him as James.' James was a normal name, a name for a regular guy. His shadow was too large for a regular name.

'Don't forget, I knew him before he was a bishop. Being a Methodist, I could never even call him Father. He was James, plain and simple. I remember when he married Julia, such a darling couple.'

'They always were. I wish they could have spent their last years together.'

'One of the nicest things about getting old is you don't waste a minute wishing. Things happen, and you deal with them. If you don't deal with them, you end up like those people on talk shows, wearing awful clothes on television.'

Clara never missed a talk show and complained bitterly about every one of them.

'Interesting.' I laughed softly. 'I was just talking to Susan about life. Is that the secret to life – deal with things?'

'Oh good heavens, Jill. Women know that there is no secret to life. Men pretend that there is one, but there isn't.' Clara seemed quite sure of herself.

'Really?' She wasn't exactly the Dalai Lama, but she was certainly old enough to have figured a few things out.

'All the philosophers are men, haven't you noticed? Women are too busy keeping life going to worry about things like that.'

'Clara, I think you might be right.' Women kept life going while men went out to slay dragons and tilt at windmills.

'I want to see more of you. Don't be afraid to come over and just sit with me if that's what you want to do. I've buried a lot of people I loved and felt different every time. Whatever you feel, whenever you feel it, it's all right.'

'Thank you. I needed to hear that.'

'I've monopolized you enough. You just sit here, like a queen, and let people come to you.' She got up and headed for the buffet table.

I did feel almost as though I were holding court. I was treated gently, with deference. Gentle touches, soft words, big white handkerchiefs, lovingly bestowed.

Chloe wandered in, and taking her cue from me, sat down and assumed her role, took on her mantle. My parents would have been proud. Gracious and warm, she remembered names, kissed cheeks, wept quietly, laughed with old men trying to charm her. Newly initiated, she was quickly learning the steps to the dance.

How often we ignore the forms, the conventions. We toss away the process that has been refined for generations and wonder why we sense a lack. We have begun to do away with funerals because they are morbid, but we have nothing with which to replace them, nothing with which to plug the holes of our grief. We want to ignore grief and can't understand why our minds feel mired in words not spoken.

Families like mine understood the process. We filled the burying grounds with granite and brownstone. We carved moon faces with angel wings, etched poignant verse. We braided the departed's hair into pictures and wore their portraits between our breasts. We built tiny houses to hold their remains. We cut sandwiches into triangles, poured aspic over the fish, opened the front door and allowed sympathy to be poured on our heads like oil. Italians had better weddings, but no one could touch us on death.

'Mom, I'm going to the airport now. Do you need me to do anything?' She stood over me, car keys in hand. I squinted at Chloe, making her face one of a granite angel.

'No, thanks for asking. If you take the Jag, it needs gas. There's a Shell card in the glove box. Don't speed.' Chloe had a lead foot, inherited from her father.

'I'm sorry for snapping at you and Aunt Susie.' Not truly contrite, but well reared.

'You didn't snap, you communicated. Now go, or you'll be late.' I stood up and kissed her smooth cheek. 'Don't speed.' I knew she didn't listen the first time, but perhaps the second?

'Yes, ma'am.' She winked at me and left the room, tossing the keys in the air and catching them. She may have learned the dance but her part of it was over for now. I knew she would go over the speed limit; it's hard not to when you're eighteen.

'Sorry I'm late, Jill. The time got away from me.' Elliott leaned over and gave me a chaste, brotherly kiss on the cheek.

'That's all right. I've missed you. You look wonderful.' At forty-seven Elliott had the youthful look that some blonds manage to retain. Tall, thin and bone pale by the end of the long winter, he looked almost ascetic. I suppose Victorian women would have swooned over his romantic, consumptive looks, but I couldn't help wishing he were a bit ruddier, a little heavier. I suspected my pants were bigger than his. Nobody would mistake me for a consumptive ascetic.

'So do you. I really wanted to get here sooner, but I had to drop Ben off at a friend's and I needed to pick up a book from my office.' Elliott taught history at the graduate level and wrote long complicated books about historical minutiae. He was also a wonderful kisser, and made my collarbone feel like an erogenous zone. He had long fingers with huge, sexy knuckles and hair did not grow out of his ears.

'Not a problem. Are you hungry?' Much as I had tried to control the urge, I always ended up offering him food. I wasn't sure if I was trying to control him or fatten him up. I leaned toward the control theory since I had at least paid for that information.

'Sure.' He was already eyeing the buffet table. Thin people are always eating, which proves there is no justice in the world. 'What are you doing later? Don't you think you should have a nap? A little time out?' He whispered the last in my ear, so I knew he wasn't concerned about my lack of rest. His voice wound down my ear canal and warmed the bit below my navel. An excellent voice indeed.

'Damn your white hide, Elliott.' That between a whisper and a growl so I wouldn't scandalize my parents' old friends. 'If you feel "tired" in about an hour, I can sneak upstairs for a while.' I felt myself blushing. The wanton daughter, practically rutting on her father's grave.

'I guarantee I will still be "tired" in an hour. I get "tired" every time I get within sniffing distance of you.' He made a show of looking at his watch. 'Shall we synchronize our watches?'

'I'll be upstairs in an hour or so. Eat some lunch, keep your strength up. I don't want to be disappointed.' I tugged at his tie.

'Have I ever let you down?' The teasing and whispering had passed.

'No, I don't think you ever have.' I reached up and kissed his cheek, enjoying the comfort of middle-aged passion.

'The buffet was wonderful, thank you for doing such a nice job.' I'd gone to the kitchen to speak with Hannah. Mary had alerted me that Hannah was annoyed with something one of the caterers had said about the layout of the kitchen and was threatening to leave. I really didn't want her to leave hurt and angry.

'Of course it's wonderful. It's sure not the first one I've done for the family. I've had enough practice. Truth be told, any fool can put out a luncheon buffet. That catering man makes it sound like the biggest thing in the world. I hate to think what you have to pay that man for lunch tomorrow.' Hannah was banging pans into the sink and muttering at the same time.

'I certainly didn't pay him to be cross with you. This is your kitchen, and I want you to feel free to tell him that. Frankly, we can serve coffee and doughnuts to everyone tomorrow. Just say the word, and I'll tell him to forget the whole thing.' I was fairly certain she wouldn't call my bluff. I really didn't think that coffee and doughnuts would cut it.

'If you don't mind me saying what needs to be said, he can stay. I don't want anybody saying we didn't do everything the way your mother would have wanted it to be. Your mother trained me how to run this house, and that's the way I run it. That man couldn't run a house like this if his life depended on it.' Hannah felt better. She had stopped muttering and banging.

'I wish we had more reliable people available. I know you can do a much better job than he will, but we're just not set up for those kind of numbers.'

'Don't worry, I won't let him mess this up.' The keeper of Wolden traditions. Hannah had arrived on Mother's doorstep, hungry and cold, when she was barely fifteen. My mother, a new bride, hired Hannah on the spot. Hannah felt my mother had saved her life and admired her to the point of adoration. She'd even asked me after my mother died if I would mind putting her own ashes on the shelf below my mother's in the family crypt. She'd cried when I agreed, grateful once again for Wolden generosity. Sadly, I doubt if my mother was ever aware of the devotion that Hannah offered all those years.

'I know you won't let anyone mess this up.' I hugged her in gratitude. I touched and hugged Hannah as often as I could because my mother never had. 'I have to get back to Mary and check on a few things. Thanks again for everything.' I gave her another quick hug and left the kitchen.

'Mary, would you please get the caterer on the phone in a few minutes? I just gave Hannah the green light to chew his ass off at will and it only seems fair to warn him.' I plopped myself down in the chair across from her desk. 'While I'm thinking about it, do we have any cash in the house?'

'Some, hold on a minute and I'll tell you how much.' Mary dug out and unlocked the small cash box we kept under a false bottom in one of the desk drawers. 'Looks like a little over three thousand but the caterer will take a check.'

'I know but we should tip everyone who serves tomorrow

and Chloe no doubt didn't stop at the bank before she came home. She probably needs cash.'

'We have enough to cover everything. Stop worrying about this little stuff, everything is under control.'

'Sorry, nervous energy. I'm preparing myself for Eleanor's arrival. Go crazy now, avoid the rush, that sort of thing.'

'I swear, Jill, if you didn't have Eleanor I think you would invent her.'

'What are you talking about? The woman is a certifiable barracuda.'

'She's your bogeyman, your thing that goes bump in the night. She's a bit abrasive, but I think she basically means well. Lighten up and develop a sense of humor about her.' Mary replaced the cash box. 'By the way, I don't believe that any agency certifies barracudas.'

'Sorry, I'm just thinking out loud. Did you get some lunch?'

'I grabbed a plate and came back in here. I still haven't reached a fair number of people about the luncheon tomorrow. I'm still working on that.'

'Bad week to die, lots of people out of town.' I yawned and rubbed my eyes.

'Tired?'

'I shouldn't be, I slept well last night.'

'Maybe you should go take a nap.'

'I might go lay down for a few minutes.' I thought of Elliott and smiled.

'Before you go up, I got a call for Chloe. When is she due back?'

'Around four unless the flight is delayed. If you want to leave before then, I can give it to her.'

'Good, I'm planning to leave as soon as Michael gets back. Let's see; here it is, this is cryptic: "I blew it and told Will, see you on Monday, Love, Mel". I suppose this will make sense to her.' Mary was back to checking items off one of endless lists.

'Oh Jesus! That girl is too stupid to live!'

'Chloe?' Mary knew that I thought Chloe was the most brilliant child in the world.

'No, her roommate Melanie. What a stupid little cow! How could she, what was she thinking of?'

'Jill, you are not the only one who is tired and I was never that good at reading minds. Take a couple of deep breaths and tell me, what are you talking about?' Mary had put down her list and was staring over the top of her glasses at me.

'Mary, "Will" is the reason that Chloe fainted last night in the chapel; she's pregnant. Chloe hasn't told him yet, doesn't know if she will at all. Damn.'

'I see. When did you find out?'

'Yesterday, when I picked her up at the airport. Two hours later, less than that, my father dies. Frankly, I've been afraid to flush the toilet, I figure the plumbing is going to go next.'

'I suppose there really isn't much of a stigma to an unwed pregnancy, not anymore at least.' The next words were left unspoken.

'There is still a stigma, don't fool yourself. The difference today is the assumption that you are stupid, irresponsible, unaware of the consequences. I'm not sure that that's much better than being sinful and immoral.' The daughters of Eve are still sinful and stupid. Adam, on the other hand is in Palm Springs for spring break.

'What is she planning to do?'

'She most likely will have an abortion, as quickly as possible.'

'I'm not the first one to make the observation, but I still wonder why it's so much easier to get pregnant when you don't want to.'

'Number 318 on the list of life.' I was muttering, Chloe's old trick.

'What are you talking about?'

'Susan and I were talking about all the stuff, all the things that must be in some manual, some guidebook, that somebody forgot to give us.'

'What stuff?' Mary completely lacked any sense of whimsy in her emotional make-up. I, on the other hand, had been chasing bits of light, movements out of the corner of my eye, whispers in the air, for as long as I could remember.

'Stuff. Why does only one sock come out of the dryer? Why won't men ask directions? Why do people eat liver? Why can you only find parking when you don't want to park? Why do you get pregnant when you don't want to? Stuff.'

'You two certainly were feeling cosmic this morning.'

'It's hard not to feel cosmic with all the shit hitting the fan at the same time around here.'

'Don't I recall something about things happening in threes? Your father, Chloe, and one more to go. I wonder what it will be.'

'How is everything today, Jill?' Michael had returned from Good Friday services and was making himself useful, making notes of floral arrangements received.

'It's been a nice day, a nice emotional wallow, people need more of those.'

'A wallow?' Another one with no sense of whimsy.

'You know, the way a pig wallows in the mud? Rolls in it, in his ears? Mourning lets you do that. I've been visiting with old friends, trying on my mother's hats, crying, laughing, a good wallow.'

'If you say so.'

'In your chosen profession, you should never take a

dismissive air with anyone. That's another thing you need to learn.'

'I wasn't trying to dismiss you, you're the one who's making light of things, it seems like you're just getting ready for another party, another diversion.'

'I am getting ready for a party, my father's last party. And who are you, or anyone else to decide the quality of my grief?' I wasn't angry, just curious. He was obviously annoyed with me and I wasn't at all sure why. I felt that last night had ended well and he was pleasant enough this morning.

'I'm sorry I said anything.'

'Too late, Father. You've already said it.'

'It seems that under the circumstances, your father's death, your daughter's situation, you would want some help, some input. I know there must be a dozen priests who would love to help you, and your daughter.'

'Including yourself?'

'If that's what you want.'

'Michael, I have spent my entire life surrounded by the wisdom of the Episcopal church. I grew up hearing endless debates about the meaning of this and that, the reality of one thing or another. I know as well as anyone what services are available, I also understand the limitations. I know what I need and the Church can't provide it right now.'

'What is it that you need?'

'I need to talk to old friends. I need to hold hands with old ladies. I need to try on hats and wonder which shoes to wear tomorrow. I need to play with my dogs and laugh with anyone who's around. I need to cry, and swear, and talk about my father, a good wallow. If it makes you feel any better, the service tomorrow is going to be the best wallow of all.'

'It's all just a formula to you isn't it? Something you were born into. The Church is just the family business.'

'I really don't care to join your little debating society, Michael. You will never understand what is in my heart, you are too young, too green, and too male.' I started up the stairs, then turned toward him. 'One more thing you can't afford to do? Never, never, judge someone else's faith. It's not your job.'

'Are you sure that you have to go right now?' Elliott lay on his back under the comforter. Thin people have trouble staying warm.

'We've been up here for two hours. I really do have things I need to see to.' I sat at my dressing table repinning my hair.

'When does Chloe leave?' He propped pillows behind his head and watched me repair my smudged make-up.

'A week from Sunday. Why?' I stood up and carefully pulled a black slip over my hair.

'I thought maybe we could get away for a few days. You might enjoy a change of scenery.'

'After Chloe leaves I'd love to go away. I'll really be ready for a break then.' I wondered about going away. Climbing up a level in commitment. Stepping into the rarified air of love and war. The pissing contest of Eros and Aphrodite.

He stood behind me and pulled two pins from my hair. He ran his hands under my slip and kissed me. 'Come back to bed. I'm still tired.'

I heard her before I saw her. The voice was harsh and nasal with an overlay of a British accent which she had acquired since moving to New Jersey. Eleanor felt her move to Bergen County, New Jersey, along with her new role as a retired doctor's wife, necessitated a change in accent. She had mentioned to me that she speaks the way she does because she is overcompensating to avoid a Jersey accent. That may be true to some extent, but her tones got plummier every time I heard them.

I suppressed a shudder as the door opened and she swept in like an old square-rigger under full sail. I watched from the shadows, forestalling the moment when I must kiss her powdery cheek and become enveloped by Calvin Klein's Obsession.

'Hello, Eleanor. How was your trip?' I tried to smile warmly but I knew my face probably gave me away. Chloe wouldn't notice, but Eleanor would. I quickly kissed the rouged cheek she offered me.

'Delightful, just delightful. Oh, look at all these flowers, everything looks so fresh. And I see you have a new butler.' Eleanor was sizing things up quickly, evaluating possessions and social position, the status insurance adjuster.

'Eleanor, this is Father Michael Blaine, from the Cathedral. Father Blaine, this is Chloe's grandmother, Mrs Holmes.' Michael shook her hand and nodded. I could see that he was amused at the butler comment and my obvious discomfiture. Blushing, I was embarrassed for my late husband and myself.

'I've never seen so many flowers, where did they all come from?' Had she really forgotten, couldn't she figure this out?

'They were sent because of my father's death.' I wondered if I would be offered condolences.

'Of course. Where will I be staying? I hope it is right next to Chloe?' Obviously my father's death wasn't as interesting as her sleeping accommodations.

'I'm putting you in my parents' room. I had assumed that Les would be joining you and that is the largest room, also the nicest.' Eleanor always expected the best, felt that she had earned it somehow.

'I brought you some pictures, Jill. I still think you need to make some changes in this house and I think the pictures will make you understand that. You really need to update things. You have some lovely things but nothing really stands out.' Eleanor studied 'design' at a community college a few years ago and fancied herself the new Sister Parrish. The pictures always featured rooms with bright color co-ordinated fabrics and lots of bleached wood and puffed up valances.

'Eleanor, I don't want anything to stand out.' I knew I'd told her this before. The house wasn't a magazine makeover or some monstrosity from Architectural Digest. 'I love this house and I love the way it looks.' She started to say something so I spoke quickly. 'Can I get you anything? A snack, a drink?' At least I could almost always distract Eleanor with the offer of drink or food.

'It is a little bit early, but I would love a Manhattan.'

'Why don't you take your grandmother's things up, Chloe and I will get her a drink. Eleanor, make yourself at home in the front room, I'll only be a minute.' I left quickly, grateful for the briefest respite.

I could hear her as I returned to the front of the house with her drink. Her voice could cut through any material, butter through a knife. She was regaling Michael with some story. Her stories were always filled with the best, the worst, the biggest, the smallest. Exceptional sensibilities, meant to be shared.

'Eleanor? Here you go. Can I get you anything else?'

'I'm just dandy, Jill. I was just telling this nice young man about some work we had done on the beach house last season. I was telling him that I couldn't believe what a bad job the contractors did and how much it cost.' Eleanor had found that by complaining about poor workmanship, poor service, poor flights, she could give everyone a clear idea about her importance and position.

'I hate to do this, but I have to run over to the Cathedral for an hour or two to check on some things for tomorrow. I know that you wanted to spend some time with Chloe, so I hope you won't mind too much.' Michael raised his eyebrows at me, knew I was lying. I winked at him, acknowledging my sin, regretting nothing.

'You go ahead. I'll be fine with the young people.'

I had no destination, just the need to escape, to drive fast. I understood the drunks, the liars, the transvestites, the suicides, all the bolters. The ultimate luxury. Do the bolters have an extra gene that allows them to escape? Surely it was a gene I lacked because I dutifully turned the car around and headed back to my life. Nothing lost, but a few dollars worth of gas, I was back in less than an hour.

'Back so soon?' Eleanor was sitting in the front room, swirling ice cubes in her glass. A movie buff, she had taken most of her mannerisms from old movie stars. I think this was a Bette Davis move.

'Everything is under control. I thought maybe we could go out for dinner tonight.' I liked to keep Eleanor in public places. I knew I wouldn't murder her in public.

'Sit down, Jill. We need to talk.' Eleanor was always talking but we never talked, just the two of us. We would have conversations, of course, but we kept them a safe distance from anything of importance.

'Fine. Where is Chloe?' I sat in a chair opposite Eleanor.

'She's upstairs with her friend Kent. She was very pleased to see him and under the circumstances I didn't see how anything could happen.'

'What circumstances? She and Kent are like brother and sister.' Susan and I had raised the two children, so close in age, almost as a group effort.

'She's pregnant, isn't she?'

'How did you know, what did she say?' I wanted to make sure she didn't say it again.

'I asked her. Women, girls, they get a different look.' This was a surprise. Eleanor had never been intuitive.

'She's just pregnant, only a few weeks. She wants to have an abortion, so I suppose she will. This is such an awful thing for her to have to deal with, to live with.'

'It's tough but it's not impossible. I had an abortion, years ago, before it was legal. It wasn't much fun but it was one of the smartest things I ever did. Have I shocked you?' For once I didn't feel that she was challenging me.

'I guess I'm a little shocked that you would tell me. We've never been very comfortable around each other.' I leaned toward Eleanor, watching her leathered face. Nearly eighty, it was hard to imagine a young woman's face under the powder and blue eyeshadow. 'I really appreciate you talking to me about this. Can I ask you a couple of questions?' I didn't want to push this, didn't want to scare either of us back into the usual pattern.

'You can ask, but I can't promise that I'll answer.'

'Do you wonder what would have happened if you hadn't aborted? Do you still think about it? I'm sorry to pry, but I want to understand. I never had one, an abortion, I mean.'

'I still think about it, but I still know that I did the right thing. The details aren't important, not now. I know what would have happened if I had had the child and it would have been a disaster.' She took a sip from her drink and stared at the toe of her shoe.

'I'm so afraid that Chloe will have to deal with this for her whole life. I'm afraid that she will never be able to put it behind her.'

'Be grateful that she has a choice. I was lucky, girls used to die all the time from abortions back then. I had a friend who was a nursing student, she found a nurse who did it for me. At least I didn't get an infection, end up in the hospital, as so many girls did.' She sat up straight and looked at me. 'She will have to deal with this for the rest of her life. Women have the longest memories in the world and most of it deals with what goes into or comes out of our vaginas. I know that you think I'm a vulgar old bag, but I've learned a few things, quite a few things. Whether it's a penis going in, or a baby coming out, you won't forget it and at some point it will break your heart.' She slammed her drink down for emphasis.

'You are a vulgar old bag, but so am I, at least I'm headed that way.' I crossed to her chair and hugged her. 'Thank you so much for talking to me.' She stiffened and I released her.

'Even vulgar old bags get hungry. I thought you were taking us out for dinner.' I helped her from the chair and we went to find Chloe.

CHAPTER SIX

We could hear them as soon as we reached the top of the stairs. The basic sound of Chloe and Kent in a room had changed through the years, but it was always loud. Four months apart in age, they were as close as most siblings, without the baggage of rivalry.

Kent was sprawled on her bed, looking at the pictures in her wallet. At eighteen, Kent was clearly his father's son. Clean chiseled features, patrician air, marred only slightly by an earring and a seven-inch flap of hair that kept falling across his face.

'Hey, Aunt Jilly. I'm sorry about the Bishop.' Kent had developed a slight southern accent at William & Mary.

'Thanks, Kent. Love the earring. When did you get to town?' Kent was the first of my godsons. Through the years I had acquired two others, but Kent remained my favorite.

'You like this? Dad hasn't seen it yet. I decided to come over here before he got home.' He ran his finger over the earring. His earlobe looked a bit red.

'Chicken,' Chloe called from her steamy bathroom. She probably had showered with the door partly open so they could talk. Like children raised together in a kibbutz, there was little sexual tension between them.

'If I get home after he goes to bed, leave before he gets up, always face North, he may not notice.' His drawl was level and unconcerned.

'Ice cream has bones, he won't notice. This is the same man who thought the Kingston Trio made a bold fashion statement.' Chloe was right. Fletch Van Houten's wardrobe had not changed substantially in thirty years. Leisure suits and Nehru collars had not changed this man's life.

'Everything is cool if I can stay out of his way for the next twenty-four hours . . .'

'Are you serious?' I never knew with Kent. I'd nursed him at my breast when he was two months old. Susan was ill and I took Kent into Chloe's nursery and under my blouse. A cuckoo in my nest, I never really gave him back to Susan. The boyness of him would always be foreign to me, but I couldn't pass him without touching him, reminding myself that he was partly mine.

'Nah, he'll be semi-cool with it. I'd already decided to take it out tomorrow, anyway. Damn thing itches like crazy.'

'I'll be ready in a minute.' Chloe came out of the bathroom buttoning up her shirt.

'Cover those up right now. There is such a thing as common decency. Damn Yankees! In the South a young lady knows the proper way to act when a gentleman is in the room.' He flopped on his back, crossing his legs and rolling his eyes. In less than a year and a half in the South, this product of three hundred years of New England spine-straightening had taken on the languor and ease of the cavalier. He seemed as Southern as the Tarleton twins who wooed and lost Miss Scarlett.

'You are such a pain in the ass, Kent. Move your goods – I'm starving and Mother is taking me and Grandma to dinner.' Chloe slapped his leg and pushed him aside so she could sit on her bed to finish dressing. Unlike Kent, she at least still seemed Yankee to the core. She pulled on wool knee socks which matched her crew neck sweater. She wore a pleated tartan skirt which she had owned for at least five years. The hair caught by a gold clip at the back of her neck, was her only adornment, the only extravagance. You will know them by their knee socks.

'Am I being kicked out?' Kent looked at me in mock dismay.

'Yes, dear. It's a hen night.' I smiled as I showed him the door. 'I'm afraid you may have to see your father tonight, after all.'

'Eleanor? May I come in?' I knocked softly on the door. Dinner had been pleasant enough and I wanted to make sure she was comfortable. If I neglected this sort of thing I got angry letters from Allison.

'Come in.' She was propped up in bed wearing a frilly bedjacket, her hair still combed up and her make-up in place. She reminded me of an elderly courtesan or one of the Gabor sisters.

'Do you have everything you need?'

'Sit down, I want to talk to you.' She pointed toward the chair next to the bed.

'Only for a bit. I've got some things I need to go over.' I shouldn't have put her in my parents' room. I resented her sitting in my mother's bed, tarted up, boozy, and overblown.

I sat down but didn't lean back or cross my legs. I had no intention of staying.

'This won't take long. We need to talk about Chloe.' She was arranging her sheets as though she were straightening a desk.

'What about Chloe?' I could feel my leg muscles tightening, my feet pulling under the chair.

'Don't try to stop her. She thinks that you will pressure her to keep the baby and she doesn't want to do that. Your child is gone and all the grandchildren in the world can't bring him back.'

'What are you talking about?' I'd almost forgotten Chloe's problems. As always, Eleanor distracted and confused me.

'Your little English brat, of course. Did you really think that your first kid was still some deep dark secret?' She looked at me with satisfaction. 'I don't care one way or the other, of course. I just want you to know that you can't expect Chloe to give you the child that you gave up. You two have got to live separate lives. You had your chance. Now she has hers.'

'Who told you about him?' There were only a handful of possibilities.

'Why, Rick told me. It was right before he died. You two had had some argument. He was very angry with you, and it spilled right out. It was all I could do not to laugh.' She was laughing now. 'The Bishop's perfect young daughter whose shit didn't stink. Just think, Jill dear, we have something in common, don't we? We were both wayward girls. Do you suppose this will make us closer? Is this what they call bonding?'

'Why are you telling me this now? I don't see any point in discussing this.' I turned to leave the room. I wished that Rick's ghost was around so I could kick it in the balls.

'This thing with Chloe has finally got your attention. You wouldn't have listened before, but now you have to. Why you're almost to the point where you can talk about how my son died.' She examined her nails and reached for an emery board on the bedside table.

'Christ's sake, Eleanor. You are talking nonsense. Can't you see I'm trying to make the best of a bad situation? Can't you see that I'm trying to do the right thing?' I was shaking and grabbed the doorknob.

'Yes, the right thing. Your family has always owned the

"right thing" franchise, haven't they? Was it the "right thing" when they "bought" my son for you? You were never his grand passion. How could you be, you little brown mouse?' Her lips pulled away from her dentures in a smile. 'Lucky for you that girl died in the crash along with him or everyone would have found out she wasn't a client.'

'She was a client. He was giving her a ride home.' Part of the catechism my father wrote for me. He said it and I repeated it. I repeated it for sixteen years.

'He'd told me about her. He was quite taken with her.' She filed her left thumbnail and compared it to the right.

'Why are you telling me these horrible lies? What do you hope to gain by lying about your own son?' I felt like my chest was being ripped in half. I tried to slow my frantic breathing.

'No lies, Jill. I didn't blame him, of course. He was almost forced into marrying you. I don't suppose it would have lasted very long if you hadn't gotten pregnant when you did. You were quite the breeder in those days, my dear.' She rolled on her side and pulled the duvet up to her ears.

'Rick loved me and he loved Chloe.' I tried to keep my voice low. 'I always hoped to find out that Rick was adopted because my one regret in life is that your blood is in my child's veins.' I had other regrets but this was a big one.

'Whatever you say, Jill.' Muffled under the covers, I could barely hear her plummy tones. I spent a moment entertaining myself with the thought of how easy it would be to suffocate her. I spent another moment wondering if it were possible to divorce a man who had died over sixteen years ago.

I held a cold washcloth to my face and tried to steady my breathing. I sat against the closed bathroom door and wrapped my arms around my knees. Eleanor's voice looped through my brain, an unstoppable drone. My brain argued with the voice until I realized she was right.

My parents had arranged for Rick just as they had arranged for my schools and summercamps. Since I was incapable of making suitable arrangements, they had been made for me. I'd never really questioned the story about the client because everyone wanted me, needed me, to believe it. It made things easier for all concerned.

For sixteen years I'd accepted the story and played my part. I'd let the world see my single state as a tribute to my love for Rick, when deep in my soul I knew what Rick had done, what he had been. Only Elliott, the man who had driven my father to the mortuary the night of Rick's death, had been allowed inside my carefully constructed life.

I locked my bedroom door and climbed into bed. The telephone was in my hand and his number was punched in before I knew what I would say.

'Sorry to call so late.' Elliott and I had never discussed that night. Sally and Elliott had come to me as soon as they heard. I could see Sally playing with Chloe, feeding her dinner. I recalled the way Elliott had tucked his hand under my father's elbow when they left to deal with what remained of my husband.

'It's all right. I was just reading in bed.' His voice was groggy and I knew I'd awakened him.

'I need to talk to you about something. I know it's late, but I really need to know some things.' I wondered if I really wanted the truth after sixteen years.

'The answer is yes.'

'What are you talking about?'

'Yes, I think those white pubic hairs are very cute. I also like that little freckle above your right nipple.'

'Elliott, please.' Phone sex had no charm for me that night. 'I need to ask you about the night Rick died.'

'Jilly, that was a long time ago.' His voice was soft and slow. 'I'm not sure I can recall much about that night, not reliably anyway.'

'Bull. You remember Richard Nixon's birthday and you're not even a Republican.' I'd been expecting this. We often spoke of Sally, but never of Rick.

'I'll try. What do you want to know?'

'First of all I want to know you will tell me the truth – the truth with no omissions.'

'Have I ever lied to you, Jill?'

'No, Elliott, you haven't lied to me, but I've never talked to you about that night. I want you to know I'm serious, I want the truth.'

'Fine. Ask away.'

'Rather than my asking specific questions, just tell me what you remember about that night.' I didn't want to ask the wrong question and give the truth another chance to slide around the corner.

'I remember being terrified.' His voice sounded strained. 'I had never known anyone my age to die. I remember thinking if Rick could die, so could Sally. I was so scared.' His voice cracked and rose. 'Jill, can't this wait? Let's talk in a few days. Get the service out of the way and let things get back to normal.'

'Eleanor told me about the girl who died with Rick. She said she'd known about her for a while.' Suddenly cold, I pulled the duvet up to my chin.

'Miserable old harridan. You know better than to pay attention to her. She's a bitch, always has been.' His voice was lively, warming to the subject. Like Susan, he knew hating Eleanor was one of my requirements.

'But is she telling the truth?' I knew he was trying to distract me. 'I need to know what you know.'

'The girl's family was at the mortuary when we got there. Her name was Sharon, some Italian last name. Her parents were devastated. They'd met Rick, but didn't know he was married.' Elliott took a deep breath before he continued. 'Your father, her parents, the firm's partners, everyone wanted to keep it quiet. Rick's car was well insured by the firm and Sharon's parents were given a large settlement. Between your father's influence with the local powers that be, including the newspaper, and the legal manoeuvrings of the firm, everything was kept very quiet.'

'Is that all of it?' Not that it wasn't enough.

'Except for my part. Your father tried to convince me that the girl's family was mistaken about Rick's relationship with their daughter. I'd always liked Rick and I wanted to believe him, so I did. It didn't seem to matter until recently.'

'Why recently?'

'When Sally died I needed to know everything. I even read the autopsy report. Her death was the last thing I had of hers and I needed to know everything I could, I needed to "own" it. You never got to do that. I can see now, I can see that you should have been allowed to deal with it then.' Sally died on a beautiful Sunday afternoon off Martha's Vineyard. Her sailing dinghy had swamped and a ski boat had come over to help her. As she swam toward the boat, the driver mistakenly went into gear. Sucked under by the boat, her chest had been opened by the propeller. Even so, Elliott had read the autopsy report.

'I'm not convinced it would have changed anything. Maybe I even knew, just couldn't think about it.' I brushed the hair off my face, surprised to find my face wet with tears, surprised by my admission.

'Can you look at it now? Can you hate Rick now?'

'What possible good would it do to hate a man who has been dead for sixteen years? I have to look at pictures to remember his face. I don't remember his voice at all. It's nothing but ancient history.'

'It's you, it's your history, Jill. Sally is finally gone for me and I want to make a life with you. I'm afraid that you won't be able to love me until you can hate Rick.' His voice cracked.

'I thought it was Sally. I've felt so many times that Sally was getting between us.' I thought of her sunhat still hanging on his kitchen wall. The beautiful pictures around his house, Sally squinting, laughing, kissing. Sally whose hair would always be ginger, whose skin would always be smooth and young.

'Sally hasn't been the problem. Sally is gone, but Rick is still messing up your side of the bed.'

'Messing up the bed and making us both sleep on the wet spot?' I wondered if I hadn't drowned in that spot years ago.

'Seems that way. Sixteen years is a long time to sleep on the wet spot, Jill.'

'You're a very wise man, Elliott.'

'I'm a wise man who loves you very much, Jill.'

'Elliott . . .' My voice choked as tears splashed on the telephone's mouthpiece.

'One more chance, then I go to a singles' bar. I love you.'

'I love you too.' I did. I also felt I'd just given something away.

CHAPTER SEVEN

I arrived at the Cathedral early. I wanted to make sure that all was as he had wanted. His instructions followed to the letter. One last time to try to meet his need for form and precision. My father had seen his need for perfection as a flaw, something almost shameful, something to hide from all but the most trusted in his life. He had known it to be wrong, a lack of generosity, a lack of compassion, yet there it was, in every minute of his day. Thousands of minor irritations and flaws only he saw. He would have made a wonderful jeweler, perhaps a diamond cutter, a cabinet maker of such skill the angels would cry.

Do we ever please the parent, do we ever stop trying? Dead almost forty-eight hours, and still his need for perfection, his need for suitability gnawed at me, nagged in my ear. Maybe it's true, maybe we only become adults when our parents die. If that's true, is the adult born or does the child die?

It stood there, so small, so hard. I knew it was going to be there but still it surprised me, shining between the explosions of flowers. The earthly remains of spirit, that awesome force confined inside a small brass urn. I wondered if it still might be warm from the terrible fire; over a thousand degrees I read once. If I walked up to it, if I stared into it, my reflection would be twisted and distorted. I backed away, not needing a closer look.

'Here, Mom, thought you might want these.' Chloe sat beside me and handed me my car keys.

'Where did you find these? They must have fallen out of my purse.' I shoved them into my bag, checking the bottom of the purse, looking for an exit point.

'You left them in the car. Are we feeling a bit distracted?'

'We are feeling ever so slightly crazed. What time is it? I forgot my watch this morning.'

'It's about half-past nine. Did you remember to wear underwear?' She pretended to check under my suit.

'Stop that. I'm afraid to look. It wouldn't surprise me if I did forget this morning – underwear, that is.'

She turned in the pew and began to look around. 'Mary is sitting in the back. Shall I go get her?'

'No you stay here. I'll go get her.'

Mary was kneeling at the built-in kneeler in front of the rear pew. I sat beside her and waited for her to finish. I suppose I could have joined her in prayer, should have joined her, but I remained seated. I looked toward the altar, the bank of flowers and the shiny little urn. When I was a child I was convinced that on the last day, the last trump would sound, and all the little vases would burst open and people would burst out whole and complete, genies out of the bottles. I used to wonder how my brothers would be dressed, would they have grown along with me or stayed little blue infants? I knew that the ground would rumble and all the stillborn pups, fallen birds, and roadkills that Susan and I had buried would leap from the back garden and frolic through the gate.

I remember where it came from, my vision of the afterlife. Some Jehovah's Witnesses had left a magazine at the door. Imagine the faith and daring of that person, to leave a copy of *The Watchtower* at a bishop's home. The cover was a graphic depiction of Judgment Day at the cemetery. A happy, vaporous family rose from the grave, holding hands and smiling skyward. It seemed much more satisfying than anything I had learned at the Cathedral. I remember sitting on my father's lap and asking him which of the vaporous ladies he thought was the prettiest. I remember hoping he would pick the one with long brown hair, like mine.

I hoped that things were as he felt they should be. I hoped that he hadn't found that God was a blue elephant, a tree in Argentina, a sham.

'What are you doing back here, Jill? People are starting to arrive.' Mary pulled me out of my musing.

'What are you doing back here? I want you up front in the family pew.'

'No, I couldn't, not today.'

'Somewhere, in all those pages of instructions, Dad must have specified you were to sit up front with us. I would consider it a favor. If you sit on one side of me and Chloe sits on the other, Eleanor can't get to me.'

'You and your bogeyman. If you insist, I would love to be next to you, thank you.' She reached for her purse, rising to her feet with a small grunt. 'It's the end of an era, Jill. He's gone but other things are starting up. This is your chance to spread your wings a little bit. Think of it as a career change.'

'What career?' I was the only forty-three-year-old American woman with a college degree who had never earned a dime. Only my volunteer résumé was impressive.

'You've made a career of being the dutiful daughter and the good mother.'

'You make me sound like such a martyr.' I hated martyrs, especially when I was the one on the cross.

'I don't think you are a martyr at all, that's not the point anyway. I think you've settled rather than chosen. It's time for you to choose what you want for a change. Your father is gone and Chloe will be fine. If she isn't fine, it's her life, not yours. Take a trip, bleach your hair, sleep with that darling Elliott who's been hanging around.' She smiled slyly. 'I've noticed the way he looks at you and I'm certain he's interested.' I wondered what Mary would think if she knew that Elliott and I had made love on her desk two weeks ago.

'Mary, we are in church.' I whispered with mock severity. I'd been touched by her concern.

'Church, smurch. Put yourself first for a while.' She patted my hand.

'We'd better move up front. The seats are getting pretty filled.' I took her arm and walked her toward the front of the cathedral.

'It's almost over, dear. Get your veil down and check your hankie supply. Let's make the old boy proud.' She squeezed my hand as we went toward the urn.

I sighed and smiled at her. I did want to make the old boy proud. I always had and always would, try to make the old boy proud. Old habits die hard.

I was glad to be holding a prayer book. The simple act of holding the familiar black book gave time a reality it may have lacked otherwise. I knew if I could feel the leather binding, the smooth gilt-edged pages, pull the satin ribbons, I was there, in the moment.

Religious services have always confused me, confounded me. I have always lost track of time, a sense of place in the pews. Perhaps that is the intent. Soaring ceilings, light filtered through colored glass, smells of wax, flower, and incense. Perhaps that is why we no longer make blood sacrifices. The smell of blood would force our minds to the present, to the now. Is there a more disturbing odor than sweat in a church?

They came in, a cast of thousands, or so it seemed. Was Busby Berkley an Episcopalian? An old friend, a gay Franciscan, says bishops have the best drag. Elegant, fabulous embroidery, stiff, sumptuous satins and silks. To die for.

That morning there were three bishops: Bishop Mark and two bishops from neighboring dioceses. They seemed to compete in grandeur, adjoining principalities flaunting their wealth, grace, and style. The service was to be the best theater that the Church had to offer. All the bells and smells, all the sights and sounds.

I've always wondered about churches with simple services – Methodists, Quakers, Congregationalists. Can you behave in an ordinary way, dress in an ordinary way, for something so extraordinary as attempting to touch God? I have a clearer understanding of the Baptists and Pentecostals. I understand why they shout and dance, speak in tongues. We seek God because we are amazed, agog, confused, because the usual no longer works. It has always seemed to me we should use the wild, the magnificent, the rare in our search.

The service lasted an hour and a half. My father's vision held and it was a rare thing of pageantry and beauty. It was a service of celebration designed by a man who knew who he was and what he believed. He had believed every word that was spoken that morning. I don't know if others knew that. To say this man had been a true believer is to call into question the beliefs of other worshippers, other clergy. To hold up his faith for its uniqueness is to imply others have considered the facts, and have found something wrong, something missing.

Bishop Mark was flawless in his performance of the Mass. A skilled clergyman must strike a delicate balance between the theatrical and the holy, between heaven and hell. Not to belittle the profession, but even Jesus turned water into wine, not vital to his message but impressive nonetheless.

I felt bereft, abandoned, cast adrift to chart my own course as an orphan, a broken thing smashed against the earth. My lungs could barely pull sufficient air, my heart strained with the effort to beat. I was grateful to be kneeling through long parts of the service, knowing my ankles could not support me.

Portions of Brahms' Requiem were sung by the cathedral choir. Beautifully performed, seemingly flawless to my untrained ear, it was the elevator music to my grief. Although sung in English, the words had no meaning to me. The poetry and assurance of resurrection; pointless because I no longer believed in promises.

Slowly, the air, the mood, shifted. Sometime during Communion I began to breathe comfortably, I felt my shoulders lower and relax, my hands unclench. The promises of comfort, redemption, eternal life and unending love once again became possibilities. The gaping maw which was my grief began to fill with purpose, with tomorrow, with Chloe, with Elliott, with me. I found myself wondering how the caterers were doing, if they were finding everything. A perpetual child, my attention span was limited to slightly less than an hour before I began to wander back to the elements of food and comfort, hearth and home.

During the distribution of the Communion, the choir began to sing 'Amazing Grace', very softly, an invitation to be joined. That fine old workhorse of a hymn; sadly neglected for decades before becoming almost a generational anthem in the sixties. This was my only addition to the service. A special request from Jill to her daddy, bon voyage. My hymn, not my father's, guaranteed to make me weep. Perhaps I had it sung so that I could be assured of crying, tangible expression of my pain, my loss.

The benediction was delivered and the clerical parade filed out. I stood and waited for Mary and Chloe to rise. Michael Blaine waited for me, his face free of expression, to lead me behind the priests and acolytes.

I could feel his arm, young and strong, through the wool and cotton of his clothing. His arm, so tangible and real stirred me and for a moment I wondered how his arms would feel around me, how his mouth would taste against mine. I found myself smiling at my own absurdity and I'm quite sure that there were comments that day about my faith and bravery. Perhaps it was a faith of sorts. A faith and bravery of species that encourages us to think of mating in the midst of grief. This was an absurdity I would never act on, I knew that beyond any doubt, but I did wonder if we were all, at heart, sluts and satyrs under a thin veneer of form and civility, ready for the rut.

Father Michael led me out of the door into the thin spring sun and led me toward the reception area across the courtyard. I held onto him, no longer aroused or amused but comforted by his size and the steadiness of his arm. I could hear his voice and knew he was talking to me, but somehow the words didn't register. I felt as though I had fallen asleep on a train and was just waking up.

'I'm sorry, Michael, what did you say?' I would really try to listen to the answer.

'Are you all right? You looked like you blanked out there for a minute.' He sounded concerned but his eyes were darting about, looking for something or someone.

'Just lost in thought for a minute. I'm sure you have things to do, feel free to do what you need to do, I'm fine.' I did feel fine, strong and fine.

'I don't see Chloe. She was behind us when we started

up the aisle, right next to Mary. I wonder where she could have gone.' He was still scanning the mourners as they left the building.

'She probably wanted a few minutes to herself. She's really not a very public person and she is uncomfortable with things like reception lines. She'll show up in a little while.'

'Let me get you inside before everyone else and then I'll go look for her.'

'I can go inside by myself, that's certainly not a problem, but you don't need to find Chloe. Trust me, she's fine.'

'I want to be sure. She didn't look very good at the end of the service.'

'Her grandfather just died and she's pregnant, which she doesn't want to be. You might not look so hot yourself. Please, just leave her alone for a while.' Priests have a terrible time understanding they aren't always wanted and needed. The young ones seem to think they are all stars in the human drama. Emergency help for the soul. Call 911 PRIEST.

'I'm sure you know best, Jill. Let's go inside.' His voice was frosty but he took my elbow and ushered me into the hall.

Something fell away from me as I walked into the reception. The worst was over, the worst was behind me. I didn't look behind me but I imagined I was leaving soft gray blobs of matter on the floor, the grief and tension left to congeal on the old oak floors.

A line quickly formed to my left and I greeted everyone who passed my way. There were very few tears but quite a few blotchy faces and damp handkerchiefs twisted in hands. Kind words were spoken and happy memories shared. So many people in the room had been touched by my father, married by him, baptized by him, counseled by him. I was struck, as perhaps I had never been, at what a remarkable man he had been. Times such as those remind us of what remarkable creatures we all are, kind, thoughtful, loving, remarkable creatures.

Coffee, tea, and tiny pastries were served at the reception. I regretted that I couldn't invite everyone to the luncheon at the palace. I loved everyone there, even those I was meeting for the first time. I'm not by nature a generous soul. I'm judgmental, a snob. I'm intolerant and I was no doubt toilet trained too soon, but on that day I was somehow transformed. By some process I don't pretend to understand, I became the person I always hoped I could be. I was warm and gracious and completely sincere. I hugged people I had just met because they had loved my father. I kissed wrinkled cheeks offered for my blessing. People lined up not just to offer me comfort but to receive my benediction as though I were a holy woman, a giver of grace.

The telling is bizarre but I actually felt as though I bestowed something almost holy that hour. My right hand began to tingle, in a very pleasant fashion and I felt as though some energy passed from me to each person. Perhaps it was a last gift from my father, the gift of being holy, if only for an hour. That hour convinced me, as my forty-plus years had not, that the man was truly gifted with some spirit most could never tap. It remains the only explanation for the reaction of the people that day. The love they had felt for my father was transferred to me. The miracle was I was able to receive it.

I was so disappointed when the crowd began to thin. I wanted everyone to stay. I was the cheerleader on prom night, feeling things would never be better than this.

'Jill, we need to think about getting back to the house. Lunch will be put out in about an hour and some of the luncheon guests have already left, so I assume they are on their way.' The tears Mary had shed, and they were copious, were gone. It was actually pleasant to realize Mary was still tracking the day, keeping me on task as no one else could.

'Sure. I just need to find Chloe to let her know that we're leaving. We came in separate cars but I need to make sure that Eleanor is riding back with someone.' All I needed was Eleanor abandoned on the side of the road.

'Eleanor is with Chloe. Father Blaine drove them back to the house in Chloe's car. Apparently Chloe wasn't doing too well.'

'What do you mean?' I was so busy I hadn't thought about Chloe since my conversation with Michael.

'She was just a bit upset. Michael got her calmed down but he thought it best to take her back and Eleanor went with them.' Mary sounded annoyed. With me, with Chloe?

'Oh God, I didn't even notice. Michael said she didn't look good but I didn't really pay any attention to him.' I had done what I had, on occasion, accused my father of: neglecting his daughter for the masses, for his flock.

'She'll be fine and Michael was really quite good with her. Besides, you were needed here and Chloe knew that, she knows that. She knows what today is going to be for you.'

'I should have taken care of her. I've spent so much time taking care of my father that Chloe has been on the back burner for the last year. At least this is the last time that he has to come first.'

'Chloe has never been on the back burner and you know it. I said it before and I'll keep saying it until you listen: put yourself first. Chloe has to have a life of her own and so do you.' She was actually pointing a finger at me and shaking it for emphasis.

'I hear you, Mary. I can't help but feel she came home needing me and I was still taking care of Dad, the funeral and all.' I shrugged my shoulders.

'None of this was for him, not really. Oh he certainly enjoyed the planning and all, but today was for you and everyone else. Everyone can feel that he is finally gone. They can also feel they have done something by being here, talking to you. Chloe understands that. She's a tough girl. She could teach you a thing or two.' Mary pulled her keys out of her purse. 'Would you like me to drive? We can always have someone bring me back for your car.'

'That's the best offer I've had all day.'

'The only thing left is the luncheon and that should be pretty easy. With the exception of His Purpleness, as you refer to him, everyone there will be old friends. Actually, I'm looking forward to it and so should you.'

'I'm looking forward to a glass of wine and taking these damn shoes off.' During the months of being housebound with my father I had gotten in the habit of wearing nothing on my feet but socks or slippers. My feet felt tortured by the black shoes I had worn that morning.

'Well you can hardly pad around the luncheon in your stockinged feet, so complete relief is still a few hours away.'

'It's my house and I will do what I damn well please.' I spoke with mock severity, enjoying the feel of the mild profanity as it crossed my lips.

'You have always been a difficult child.' Mary hugged me and we walked toward the car.

CHAPTER EIGHT

As Mary had predicted, some of the luncheon guests had already arrived. The driveway to the house was narrowed with cars parked to the right and people were beginning to park on the street. A young priest whom I recognized from the service saw the car and directed us in.

Father Michael seemed to have resolved the most immediate problems with Chloe because he was stationed at the front door with what I assumed was the guest list. Two other young clerics were providing what seemed to be a valet service of sorts. For all the world it looked like an old-line WASP version of a scene from a Godfather movie.

'Michael, Father.' I ran up the steps and nodded to the young men. 'How is Chloe, what happened?'

'Emotional overload is probably the best description. She's fine now, I think. She brightened up as soon as we got in the car. She's been greeting the guests and checking with the caterers.' He was smiling, clearly taking responsibility for her improvement.

'Thanks Michael, I owe you one.' I stood on my toes and kissed him briefly on the lips. I didn't wait for his reaction but went inside with Mary

Chloe's face brightened when she saw me, and she approached, looking refreshed and calm. She stopped to direct one of the waiters serving drinks, reminding me of a young chatelaine.

'I'm sorry I ducked out, Mom. I just needed to get out of there, forgive me?' She smiled her most dazzling smile and cocked her head slightly, a trick from her toddlerhood which still worked.

'Nothing to forgive, sweetie, I was just worried about you. Are you all right now?'

'I feel fine, better than, actually. The caterers are doing a great job and everything is on schedule. The buffet should be ready in about fifteen minutes and Mike says about half the guests are here.'

'Good girl. Do me a favor and toss these into a closet.' I stepped out of my shoes and wiggled my toes. 'One more thing, get me a glass of wine and make sure it's full. I haven't been drunk in years and today just might be the day.'

'Will do. Don't worry about a thing, I'll take care of you today.' She was clearly enjoying the idea of role reversal.

'I will accept any and all TLC that comes my way today. Is there anybody neglected, anyone I need to see to right now?' Most of these people had known each other for years so I knew I didn't have to go through endless introductions.

'Elliott is in the library looking uncomfortable. He's not talking to anyone and he's pretending he's interested in the books.'

'What about Ben?' I was worried about the effect of the Mass on the motherless boy.

'He's fine. We cadged him a snack from the caterers and he's playing with the dogs. He's a pretty cool kid.'

'He is a neat kid. Thanks for your help.' I gave her a brief hug. 'I'm going to go find Elliott and see how he is doing.' Like Ben, Chloe was ignorant of the newer dimensions of our old friendship.

'Elliott?' His back was to me as he studied the books in my father's library.

'Hi, Jilly. I was just looking for a book your dad had mentioned to me. I'll be out in a few minutes.' His voice was high and strained.

'Come here.' I pulled his hand and faced him toward me. His fair skin was slightly mottled and his eyes were still wet. 'Oh, Elliott.' I put my arms around him and rested my head against his chest. Slowly he raised his arms, returning my embrace.

'Sorry. This is the first funeral I've been to since Sally's.' I felt him gulp air. 'It brought everything back.'

'I know, it does that.' I stroked his back and smiled up at him.

'I meant what I said last night. I love you very much.' He tightened his grip and kissed the top of my head. 'After we hung up last night I lay in bed, considering the possibilities.'

'What possibilities?' I pulled away slightly, looking up at him.

'The two of us. We've got two kids, two houses, two dogs, three cats. Endless possibilities. Do you suppose that you're still fertile?'

'Christ, Elliott! My father's funeral was this morning, I've got one hundred people coming for lunch, and you want to know if I'm fertile.' I felt warm and happy, and yes, fertile.

'Just considering possibilities.' His hand wandered under my jacket.

'Chloe thought something was wrong.' I slapped his hand down.

'I thought coming into the library was better than telling her that I wanted to feel up her mother before lunch.'

'You'd been crying though.' I had developed a powerful thirst for the truth in the last hours.

'Partly relief, darling.' "Darling" was a new endearment and I liked it. 'I've been wondering for weeks if I should talk to you about Rick's death. I had hoped that your father would have told you years ago. I've been afraid to ask you how much you knew.'

'Once my father swept something under the rug, it stayed there.' My son had never been mentioned. No doubt my father had prayed for his grandson daily. He would have discussed him with God.

'Well, it's out and it's over. Ancient history.'

'You're being awfully dismissive for someone who's speciality is history.'

'More interested in biology right now.' He ran his hands along my hips.

'Later.'

'Later when? I feel like we're a couple of sixteen-year-olds who have to sneak around to make love.'

'Spend the night tomorrow? Isn't Ben staying with Sally's parents for spring break?' I thought it would be hard to sleep on only one side of the bed, but I was willing to try.

'Perfect. Easter services, dinner at Susan and Fletch's, and then back here for hours of sexual abandon.' His hands had once more wandered under my jacket.

'Sounds lovely.' I thought about locking the library door and ripping his clothes off, but it seemed somehow inappropriate, considering the circumstances.

'It will do for starters. We'd better join the throng out there.' He removed his hands from underneath my jacket and smoothed my suit around me. 'Before we leave you should try to get that look off your face. It's bad enough that I'll be walking around with a boner the size of Nebraska.'

'What look?'

'You look beautiful, like a woman in love.' And I was.

The luncheon was almost festive. Grief admitted and spent earlier, the focus had shifted to golf, garden, gossip, and food. The buffet table was attacked as though the guests hadn't eaten in weeks. Something about a funeral gives one a hearty appetite. Perhaps knowing that the Grim Reaper has passed over your head does something to the hunger center in the brain. I tried everything and found it delicious. I wondered how the caterer felt, seeing his work, his art, reduced to shattered carnage in under two hours.

The first and the last guests to leave were gone within twenty minutes of each other. The second round of activity had begun as the caterers dismantled the buffet and smiled quickly at me as I walked into the room. At catering school you are taught to indicate 'get the hell out of our way' with a quick smile and a nod of the head. After the third waiter gently elbowed me aside, I went upstairs to change my clothes.

'Mom? Can I come in?' She was in the middle of the room before the words were out of her mouth. 'What are you doing?'

I was trying to find a pair of pants that still fit but I was too embarrassed to tell her that. It was bad enough that she had walked in while I was trying, without success to pull up the zipper on a pair of gray flannels. 'I'm just getting comfortable.' As comfortable as a heifer in a gunny sack.

'I wanted you to know that Will called during the luncheon. Melanie told him that I'm pregnant.' She didn't sound overly surprised.

'Sorry, I forgot to give you a message from Melanie. She called to tell you that she had spilled the beans. What did he have to say?' Bullseye?

'He wants me to get counseling and either keep the baby or put it up for adoption. He thinks abortion is murder. He thinks his sperm and his balls are golden.' If nothing else I had taught her to turn a phrase.

'They all do. He sounds like the All-American boy to me. Did he offer to carry it for nine months, too?' I pulled a long sweater on quickly so that I could attempt to squeeze into another pair of pants in the privacy of my own clothes.

'Will was adopted at birth and feels like that is a perfect solution. I gather his parents are very strong right-to-life types and he's bought the whole program. I told him to go fuck himself.'

'Not very original, but I'm sure he got the idea.' I pulled an old pair of stretch pants with an elastic waistband out of the drawer.

'Aren't you going to argue with me? Fight for the unborn and all of that?' Chloe flopped on the sofa.

'You've got to handle this Chloe. At first I wanted to manage this for you, at least advise you, but you need to do what you have to do.' Success, the pants still fit.

'That's it, deal with it?' She groaned in mock distress.

'That's it. Deal with it. Do what you can live with because you have to live with it. You know what you want to do with your life and you have to figure out if a baby can fit into it.' I kissed her on the top of the head and sat on the sofa across from her.

'Well, I can't imagine handing a baby over and knowing I'd never see it again. Besides, there are too many weird people out there so I won't consider adoption. That leaves me with two choices.'

'Good, you've made a third of a choice.' No longer agonizing about telling her about my own history, I simply didn't want to clutter her life with my own.

'What did Grandmother always say? "Well begun is half done." I guess I'm half done.'

'Actually, I think Mary Poppins said that, but it's true enough. It feels good to have at least something out of the way, doesn't it?' I wasn't sure which something I was referring to but things seemed to be shifting. The icebergs were flowing again. The funeral was over, Elliott loved me, and Chloe was coping. I suppose I should have bought a lottery ticket, such was my luck.

'It does feel good. By the way, why didn't you tell me that you and Elliott are an item?' She cocked her head, looking pleased with herself.

'Who told you we were?' I cocked my head back at her in imitation.

'Ben told me. Sometimes he listens in on your conversations.'

'Oh shit.' I thought we had been so careful.

'Big deal. This is perfectly respectable. It's not as though this is some adulterous affair. I think it's neat. So does Ben.'

'Well, I'm glad that you approve, but I hate to think that Ben listens to our conversations.' Did I ever. Elliott and his phone sex. 'I also don't want Ben to think of me as a potential mother. Elliott and I have a long way to go. That's why we have tried to be discreet.' The operative word was tried.

'Well I think he's handsome and sexy and you have my blessing.' My daughter, the reincarnation of Pope Joan.

'Don't get too excited or get yourself measured for a maid of honor's dress. This could blow over next week.' I was the one I didn't want to get excited.

'Neither one of you is exactly the "blow over" sort. I think I'll start calling him "Dad".' She winked at me.

'And I'll call you "mud"! This is the first man I've managed to attract in sixteen years and you're trying to scare him off.' I kissed her cheek then wiggled deeper into my cushion, thinking of Elliott's hands.

'I couldn't scare him away if I tried, which I won't. Mom, I do have something to ask you. Can I ask you a question?'

'Shoot, but avoid vital organs.'

'This is a vital organ kind of question, I'm afraid.' So was I. 'Did you ever have an unplanned pregnancy, or think that you did?'

'Yes dear, I did.' She wouldn't force it if I chose not to tell. There are certain advantages in being WASPs.

'I just wondered.'

'Do you want the whole story? I'll tell you about it if you really want to know.'

'Was I that baby?' She sounded like she was five years old.

'Is that all you wanted to know?' I turned to look at her. I couldn't believe I was getting off the hook that easily.

'That's all I want to know.'

'Chloe, you were the most wanted baby in the history of mankind. We adored you from the moment I realized that I had missed my period. I was even excited about morning sickness, for the first day or two, anyway. No, that pregnancy had nothing to do with you.'

'It must have been wonderful, to feel that way.'

'It was. It was an amazing way to feel. I loved every single minute of it.'

'I envy you.' She muttered slightly.

'Someday you'll feel that way too. I'm sure of it.' I smiled at her as I slipped on my socks. Socks are wonderful. You can almost never get too fat for socks. 'Where is your grandmother? I just realized I haven't seen her since lunch.' I'd gone through one funeral and two receptions without saying a word to her. A record.

'I had Mike take her to the airport. I told her I would see her sometime this summer.' She moved to my dressing table and began to braid her hair.

'This summer? I thought she was planning to go to your graduation.'

'I told her I didn't want her there.'

'Why? She's the only grandparent you've got left.'

'I thought it would be better if we didn't see each other for a while. I told her I still love her, but I didn't want to see her for a few months.'

'Chloe, I really think you—'

'I really think she is my grandmother and I will determine, with her, the extent of our contact.'

'You're absolutely right.' I was ashamed at the smile I could barely suppress. Eleanor had done it this time. 'I won't mention it again.'

I wandered into the kitchen, to Hannah. My old friend, Hannah was a reminder that day. It didn't begin and end with me. She was as much a part of my history as the palm of my hand, the old report cards in the attic. The house itself seemed more complete with her in place.

'Good to see so many people there today, Jilly.' The caterers were gone and we sat at the old table over coffee.

'I'm glad they came and I'm glad they are gone. Do you realize that this is the first time in months this house hasn't been full of people? Between nurses, delivery people and the prayer warriors I feel like I've been living in the Howard Johnson's on the parkway.' I was rotating my ankles to get the blood circulating in my feet.

'You should be glad all those people were around to help you.' Hannah reminded me I was ungrateful by nature.

'I am glad they were around and now I'm glad they are gone. I like having room to swing my arms.' Swing my arms, walk around naked, eat potato chips for breakfast.

'Don't swing them too far, you still have Chloe, and Mr Claridge will be hanging around.' How had she figured out about Elliott? Had Chloe said something?

'What about Elliott Claridge?' Hannah could have taught the CIA a thing or two, and I was always interested in her sources.

'When I was at the A & P I ran into his latest house-keeper, Theta Poole? By the way, that man has no sense when it comes to hiring help. Theta Poole is a terrible gossip and I wouldn't be surprised if the whole town knows about you two.' Hannah never gossiped, she dispensed information. She was the *New York Times* and Theta was the *National Enquirer*.

'I have never even been there when Theta has been around.' No sense in denying anything, but I had been careful to avoid Theta. A life-long resident of this burg, I was familiar with the household help and their smoke signals and tom-toms. Imagine a line of white-clad women in carpet slippers and cardigans beating out the news of the day on drums and searching the sky for puffs of smoke and you will understand why I had tried to avoid Theta.

'Theta does the cleaning and she washes the sheets.' Hannah took a sip of her coffee and looked at me over the rim.

'She checked his sheets?' I wondered if she looked at them or sniffed them. 'I give up. How did she figure out it was me?'

'That part was pretty easy. I guess you would take the dogs with you when you went out to the Claridge place. Theta kept finding dog hair and paw prints on the kitchen counters. I told you Russell wasn't very well-behaved.'

'Lots of people have dogs. Why did she decide it was me?'

'Most people don't take their dogs with them to visit, not big dogs like yours, anyway.' Sherlock Holmes had nothing on these women.

'Well I guess we've been caught. Tell me, does everyone approve?' They weren't simply an investigative unit, after all.

'Oh, I think so. I know I approve. You've been alone way too long and most men can't stand to be alone at all. Unless something is wrong with them.'

'Well I'm relieved. It will be a comfort to Elliott as well.'
I wasn't being sarcastic, he probably would be relieved. His
family's roots were as deep as mine.

'Those people did a nice job on lunch today. I was real
pleased.' She had to change subjects or find herself guilty
of gossip.

'They did do a nice job.' It was partly their fault that I
couldn't get into my pants. 'It looks like they left the
kitchen in good shape too.'

'They did, indeed. That reminds me, what are you planning to do about this house? It deserves to be taken care of
properly.'

'Looking for a job?'

'If I were twenty years younger I would be.' She settled
her bulk back into the chair. 'These days I'm knocked out
by being here a couple of days.'

'Well, keep your ears open. I don't think I could get
used to somebody living in, but it would be nice to have the
same person each time.'

'House is too big for one person. In your mother's day it
would seem wrong not to have somebody downstairs, living
in. Makes it nicer for everybody. The family has help and
the help lives cheaper. Nothing but a waste, one person in
this big house.' Hannah was most likely concerned about
what the other members of the housekeepers' mafia would
think. She wouldn't want any of them to think she and
George had put me off live-in help, even though they had.

'I know how you feel, but I don't need that much help.
I'd just like to have the same person fifteen or twenty hours
a week.' I hated the responsibility of keeping someone else
busy day in and day out. Unlike my mother and grandmother, I had never been comfortable with the quasi-family
status of servants.

'If you married Mr Claridge you'd need somebody then.
Not that his house isn't real nice, but I can't see you living

in it. He'd need to come here with the boy.' Hannah reached across the table and poured more coffee into my mug.

'I'm glad you're planning ahead, Hannah, because I'm certainly not.'

'You better plan ahead, Jill. You're not old, but you're not exactly young.'

'Thanks for the reminder.'

'You're welcome. Glad you can still listen to advice.'

CHAPTER NINE

'Morning, Mom, Happy Easter.' Chloe came into my room with Russell banging in after her.

'Happy Easter to you, too.' I tried to focus my eyes and sound enthusiastic. Meggie, on the floor beside me, didn't bother to lift her head. Like me, she was not fond of mornings and had little patience with those who were. 'What time is it?' I groped for my bedside clock.

'It's about seven. I've got your coffee going and I thought maybe we could have breakfast together?' Imagine, thinking that breakfast is a social opportunity.

'Gag. We're having brunch at Susan's. Why don't you bring me coffee, climb in bed, and pretend that we had breakfast?' I believed in compromise.

'I'll be back in a minute. Don't fall asleep, I want to talk to you.' She left the room with Russell dancing behind her, while Meggie and I glared at her back, mentally cursing her for dragging us into the day.

'Mom, I've been up half the night and I've come to a decision.' At least she'd waited until I'd finished one cup of coffee.

'I'm waiting.' I took a deep breath and looked at her.

'Having a child would be a terrible mistake for me and for the child. I'm going to have the procedure, the abortion. Someday I'll be ready for this but I'm not ready for it now.' Her voice was low and controlled.

'It is the right thing to do. I realize that now.' I hugged her as close as I could while Russell tried to pry us apart with his large black head. 'I'm sorry that you have to go through with this and I hope to hell you don't go through this again. Remember it's not the mistakes you make but what you learn from them that is important.' Perhaps I could get a job writing greeting cards. Hallmark probably had a card for an abortion. I'd send them a résumé.

'This will never happen again. Never. I'm going to call Will later today and tell him what I've decided. I would rather deal with him over the phone than in person.'

'What happens when you get back to school? Won't you have to see him?'

'Not unless I want to, and I don't. We owe each other nothing, nada, zippety do da.' She yanked on Russell's ear for emphasis. 'I'll have the abortion in about a month and then I think I will become a nun since all men are dickheads.'

'They're not all bad, you might hold off on your vows of celibacy for a year or two.' Celibacy wasn't all it was cracked up to be. Now that I had been reminded of the alternative I was amazed that I'd spent the last sixteen years with my knees squeezed together.

'We'll see. Right now I'm not interested in anything with testosterone.' She glanced in my coffee cup then poured me more.

'I've been thinking. If you want to schedule the procedure for the week you graduate I can be with you. We could take a room at that nice place we stayed in last year, remember? You might like a little mothering when it's all over.' Last year it had been her wisdom teeth, this year a procedure. I liked the word, a clean and careful word. My little girl was growing up.

'Would you? I didn't want to ask, I know how you feel.'

'How I felt. I was really looking at what was best for me. You've made the decision that's right for you, that's the important thing.' I felt like a good mother with this short speech.

'I'll be glad when it's all over. I hope we can do an end run around the baby savers.'

'What are you talking about?' Living three thousand miles apart had changed her words, her voice. Her phrasing was no longer my own.

'These anti-abortion, Operation Rescue types hang out at the clinics, throwing models of aborted fetuses and screaming at you as you walk in. Good Christian folks doing the Lord's work.'

'Forget that. I'm sure we can find a private obstetrician who can do it in his office or a hospital.' I could see us running through a terrible gauntlet of housewives in 'Jesus saves' sweatshirts, backed up by angry men, shaking their red fists at us.

'I've done my research and the clinics are my only choice. There aren't many doctors willing to take the risk anymore. You must have read about the poor guys they killed because they perform abortions? These guys are taking their lives in their hands these days.'

'Let me call my doctor. She can either recommend someone or she'll know someone who can. I don't want you going to one of those places, there have to be other options.' One thing that money usually can buy is a bit of privacy.

'By all means, give it a try. I called every place I could think of and it was always the same story. The clinics are the only places willing to do it.'

'Then have it done here. Even if my doctor doesn't normally do them, I'm sure she will help you.' I sounded like my mother. She hadn't questioned the story of Moses because she was convinced that she, too, could part the Red Sea. It was really just a question of knowing who to call.

'That would mean I would have to come back here and drag it out another week. I want this done as quickly as possible. I know that might sound dumb but it's the way I feel.'

'I don't think it sounds dumb at all. We'll both feel better when this is behind you.' I patted her hand. 'I will talk to my doctor tomorrow though, she might have some other ideas.'

She came up behind me as I sat at the dressing table adjusting my hat. She held the neck of her robe with one hand as she began poking through my tray of earrings.

'Better get your clothes on, dear. We need to leave in about fifteen minutes.'

'I'm just looking for some pearls, I left mine at school. All I have to do is toss on my dress.' She held a pearl, swirled with small diamonds, up to her ear. 'Can I wear these?'

The earrings were a pair Rick had given me right after Chloe's birth. Dainty and valuable, they had little appeal for me now.

'I'd like for you to have them, I always meant to give them to you.' I wanted her idea of her father to be valuable, sparkly. His betrayal had been against me, not her.

'Thank you, they're beautiful, but don't you have one of your rules about diamonds?' She slipped them into her ears and admired the effect in the mirror.

Chloe was referring to the fashion rules she felt I alone observed. There were a goodly number of them: a woman over forty can't wear hair below her shoulders, white shoes must never be worn before Memorial Day or after Labor Day, no white shoes in San Francisco or New York whatever the date, no bare shoulders on a girl under seventeen.

'There was a rule about no diamonds before six o'clock or before the age of twenty-one. It seems to be generally flouted.' None of the usual stuff seemed to work these days.

'All your fashion rules are flouted, Mom. I'd venture a guess you are the only one who even knows what they are anymore.'

'That is the world's loss, daughter of mine. I'm going to throw convention to the wind because I was given those earrings on the best day of my life, the day you were born. I remember telling your father I would give them to you some day.' I smiled at the memory of the new family, my new family. I'd loved the bastard so much. I was so new in those days. So grateful that a wonderful man could love me. So relieved to get a second chance.

'Thank you, I love them. I'm going to keep them here. Things tend to "walk" in the dorms.' She kissed my cheek.

'I'll keep them for you.'

She headed for the door. 'Thanks again for the earrings.'

'Let's start a tradition, Chloe. Give them to your daughter or granddaughter on her eighteenth Easter?' I still intended to spend my dotage with grandchildren at my knee.

'It might be a hundred years away, but I'll remember.' As she left the room smiling I couldn't help wondering what else she might remember for a hundred years.

The seasons can change quickly here. After weeks of winter's refusal to leave, spring had pushed its way through. The day looked the way Easter morning should: bright, clean, the sun casting soft yellow light across the landscape. The car surged toward the church along roads lined with soft, mossy grass and the buds of wildflowers.

St. Swithin's is an anachronism. A wonderful old brooch, in a box of costume jewelry. When first built, the church lay on the outskirts of town, surrounded by small farms and pastureland. Since the end of World War II, ugly subdivisions have overtaken the countryside, pushing against the church property. Ungainly high ranch boxes and faux colonials with tidy yards seem ready to pounce on the old stone building, to gobble up her old rose gardens.

We arrived late, sliding into the last remaining seats, which were in the front row, just as the choir began to proceed. I glanced back and caught Susan's eye on the other side of the aisle. She winked and cocked her head, indicating Michael Blaine sitting in the pew behind her. Beside him sat Susan's son, Kent, and his two younger brothers. Apparently she had tired of flirting with the young priest and had assigned him to the children's pew, and children's status.

Ben came up the aisle carrying a large brass cross which he almost pitched like a javelin into its anchor, near the altar. Elliott sat a few places in front of the Van Houtens, looking brown and autumnal in his professorial tweeds. He got up quickly and joined us in the front pew. I wanted to lean over and bite his earlobe, but contented myself with squeezing his hand and moving my thigh to rest against his.

I'd always loved Easter, and never more so than that morning. The bright, fresh colors, the shining faces, patent leather shoes, stupid hats, white lilies, stuffed animals, and chocolate eggs all seemed extraordinary that morning. I, who had seemingly spent the last many months in dark and somber Lent, reveled in the familiar hymns and the resurrection homily. Knowing that I am almost tone deaf, I usually do little more than mouth the words to songs but that morning, to Chloe's obvious embarrassment, I sang with gusto and fervor, joy and abandon.

Outside the church, the service over, I accepted condolences and concerned offers of help, reassuring everyone

that I was fine and my father was in His Heaven. I became
the comforter, my measure of grief had been spent and the
void filled with relief and renewal.

The Van Houten's home is a 1920 colonial set on several
acres, tucked behind hedges and trees on a quiet street.
Susan, the ultimate nester, began adding to the house with
her first pregnancy. The front of the house has changed little but the rear of the house has a decidedly contemporary
feel, with its great expanses of glass and wooden decking.
Although well planned, and carefully executed, the house
has lost its focus, grown too large and ungainly, the beauty
spent at the front with nothing left for the back. We were in
the bright, sunny kitchen while Susan was finishing prepa-
rations for brunch and I was getting in her way.

'Well, the pressure should be off now.' I took a sip of
champagne, enjoying the bubbles tingling in my mouth.
I'd filled Susan in on my conversation with my daughter. 'I
know I feel a hell of a lot better now that I'm not trying to
manipulate things.'

'Jill, my dear friend, my soul sister, you are still trying to
manipulate things, it's your nature.' Susan refilled my glass
from a bottle on the counter.

'What do you mean?' I wasn't offended, just curious.

'Let me guess. I bet you've offered to be there when
she has the abortion. You've offered to pull strings to get
it done better, faster, whatever. You are probably, as we
speak, planning some gift to give her when it's all over.
You are going to turn this into some kind of mothering
event.'

'You couldn't be more wrong.' I took another sip of the
champagne. 'I gave her some earrings this morning, the
ones Rick gave me when she was born.' Caught out, I
smiled at my old friend. 'I don't really want to orchestrate
this, but I don't want her to go through what I did. I want

her to walk away from this older and wiser, not all beat up.'
I could have added, 'like I was'. It hung in the air between
us.

'She's already beaten up by it. Abortion is not an eraser.
She won't forget this, she can't. If you want her to be older
and wiser because of it, give her a chance to live it. Don't
try to ignore it or live it for her. It's not over until it's over.'

'It is over, for me at least. Ever since I found out, I've felt
I had to choose between what was best for my daughter and
that little clump of cells. If it was born, she might lose the
best years of her life, I see that now.' I saw it but I didn't
want to look at it. 'I've made my peace with it, and I think
Chloe has too.'

'Actually the whole thing has really made me think. I've
talked to my three older kids about sexual responsibility so
much in the last couple of days, they're starting to run
when I open my mouth.' She picked up her glass and
drank half its contents. 'It has scared me half to death. I
know Kent is sleeping with that girl, the brunette from
Charleston.'

'How do you know? Did he tell you?'

'He told his father. Fletch and Kent went out for some
male bonding thing last night. Of course Fletch just thinks
it proves how manly his son is but it scares me.'

'I know. It's really too bad that we all stopped being
ashamed of sex. When I was fourteen I couldn't figure out
why anyone would even want to have sex. Maybe we could
start a campaign, like they have to stop smoking. You could
show pictures of stretch marks and cracked nipples.' Sex is
wasted on the young anyway.

'How about pictures of middle-aged men scratching
their scrotums?' Susan laughed and leaned against the
counter.

'Oh please, not before lunch.' I was beginning to feel
light-headed from the champagne.

'Speaking of middle-aged scrotums . . .' I recognized the signs, Susan was on a roll.

'Must we?'

'We must. Elliott couldn't get into your pew fast enough this morning. Does this mean you two are finally going public?' She gave me her knowing, Madonna smile.

'We pretty much have to. The housekeepers have figured it out and Ben listens in on our phone calls.'

Susan had obviously planned more than the menu for this brunch. Place cards, decorated with tiny rabbits rendered in watercolors, placed me between Fletch and Elliott. She had placed Chloe and Father Michael at the far end of the table with her six children and Ben, separating them from the adults. Incurable romantic that she is, she no doubt had decided that they would be 'right' for each other. I noticed that she had even placed Kent, a possible diversion for Chloe, three chairs away from her.

The younger children picked at the adult fare. Already full of Easter chocolate, they were excused. Chloe, Michael, and Kent left shortly to hide eggs for the hunt which would take place, more out of the adults' need for tradition than the children's desire to find hard-boiled eggs in the damp yard.

Fletch emptied the last of the fifth bottle of wine into Elliott's glass, resting his hand over mine as he upended the bottle. 'How are you holding up, Jill? What are you on the stress-o-meter, about a thousand?'

'I'm fine, Fletch. Thanks for asking, but things seem to be sorting themselves out.' Everything is quite sortable when the afternoon has been spent eating salmon mousse, spring lamb and baby vegetables, washed down with three kinds of wine.

'I'm really pleased to see you two together. Been single

too long, both of you.' Fletch smiled his blessings on us.

'We're still single, Fletch.' I glanced at Elliott, wondering what he and Fletch had discussed while I stood in the kitchen with Susan.

'I know, I know. I was just thinking how much fun it would be to watch you two start fresh. Makes me feel twenty just to think about it.' Fletch put his glass on the table, sloshing wine across his hand. 'Damn.'

'Fletch. You've had two or three too many.' Susan took her napkin and dabbed at his hand.

'It's a special occasion, love of my life.' He lifted her hand and held it to his lips. 'Nimrod Claridge over there has that old twinkle in his eyes. Maybe we should do a little farming ourselves. I'd like a redhead this time.' He belched softly into his fist.

'Fletch, please.' Susan turned away and turned toward me.

'It would please me. I miss the babies. I miss watching you nurse.' He laughed and pushed his glass away. 'Children keep us young. You girls could be pregnant together. Be just like old times.'

'I'm not a girl, Fletch, and neither is Jill.' Susan rose and began to gather the luncheon plates. As she turned toward the kitchen I saw tears in her eyes.

'Where's Kent?' I saw Chloe and Michael, leaning over the deck railing watching the children hunt for eggs.

'He's on the phone with Mary Claire – that's her name, Mary Claire. God that is so Southern. Why not just call her Miss Lillian and get it over with?' Susan was having trouble with her son's first serious romance.

'What did you think would happen when we sent him to a southern school? Maybe it's time we had a little of that sweet feminine charm in this family. My dear, we are just too Yankee.' Fletch nuzzled Susan's neck.

'Stop chewing on me, Fletch! I feel like a bone when you do that.' An old game of theirs I had watched many times. Sadly I recognized a bite in Susan's voice, a hard edge, perhaps based on my new information about them. I wished she had never told me, burst my bubble.

'Nothing wrong with hard-headed Yankee women, Fletch. They civilized this country and birthed you and me. Imagine the world without the Abigail Adamses, the Harriet Beecher Stowes, the Eleanor Roosevelts, not to mention the fine examples of the breed we see before us on this fine day.' Elliott made a partial bow in my direction.

'Much as Susan and I appreciate being lumped with Abigail Adams and Eleanor Roosevelt, I for one don't see myself as some sort of prototype Yankee woman.' Apparently the wine made him as warm as it did me, since he was waxing eloquent about the charms of Yankee women. Not that I didn't think that as a group, we were superior in every way to every other group of women in the world. I would never admit that, unless I was convinced the listener would agree with me. I could love Elliott just because of the way he felt about my breed. I wondered if Elliott was wearing those black boxers I liked so much. Wonderful legs on that man.

'But just look at the three of you.' He was including Chloe and Michael in the discussion. 'The fine-boned beauty, the graceful limbs, the fiery intellect, the iron will, the subtle fashion sense. God, you are all great.'

'Susan, I need to know where you got that wine, I want to pour it into the water system.' I wanted to chew on his earlobes again and I hadn't been able to chew on his earlobes all day.

'Dad! Look, over here!' Ben held up a basket overflowing with bright eggs and foil-wrapped candy.

'Great, are you going to share?' He waved and Ben ran off looking for more.

'He is the greatest kid, Elliott.' Darker than his father, more Sally than Elliott. I'd loved him when I still merely liked his father. I squinted at him and wondered how a child of mine and Elliott's would look. Nimrod Claridge, indeed.

He put his arm around my shoulder and gave me a gentle squeeze. 'At least one more where that came from, darling.'

I finished my glass in one gulp.

CHAPTER TEN

I carefully layered cold meat left from the reception the day before onto slabs of white bread. The dogs stood at my feet, cheerfully assuming I would slip and the whole platter of leftovers would crash to the floor. Considering the amount of wine still sloshing through my veins, their assumptions were not unreasonable.

'Do you want mustard?' I turned to Chloe who stood in the doorway.

'Sure. Do you need any help?'

'You can get the plates and whatever you want to drink. I'll just have some tea.' I was hoping the tea and protein would replace whatever brain cells I'd lost during the afternoon.

'Coming right up. Why did Elliott and Ben leave in such a hurry?' She pulled clean plates out of the dishwasher.

'He had to run Ben to the airport. Sally's parents live in Florida now and Ben is spending his spring break with them.' I carried the sandwiches to the table. 'I think that's everything.'

'Looks good. Is Elliott coming over later?' She sat down and unfolded a napkin on her lap.

'I wanted to talk to you about that.' I wasn't sure how to

discuss my overnight plans with my daughter. 'Since Ben is out of town . . .'

'Say no more. I'm not to come into your room at seven in the morning with the dogs. Right?' She reached for a sandwich.

'I hope you don't mind, but this is the first real chance we've had to be alone. Overnight, that is.' I felt the color rising in my cheeks.

'Mother, please. This is quite acceptable. Sex is beautiful and normal. Loving relationship, consenting mature people. Do I have to recite the lecture you've given me since I could remember?'

'This whole conversation seems very weird.' I bit into a sandwich to keep myself from talking.

'Elliott is a great guy. Just take it slow. I'd hate to see you jump from taking care of Grandpa to baking bread for Elliott.'

'I'm not much of a bread baker.'

'You know what I mean. I overheard the bit about Nimrod Claridge and farming. He wants to marry you and fill you up with a menopausal baby. Is that what you really want?' She threw her sandwich to Russell who swallowed it in one bite.

'We are simply talking. I must admit I find the idea of a baby tantalizing, if you will. Maybe it's just the idea I like.' I liked the idea of my breasts filled with milk. I liked the idea of a downy head on my shoulder. I liked the idea.

'You'll show me, won't you? You'll show me who the real woman in this house is.' Chloe stood up and carried her plate to the sink.

'Chloe, this has nothing to do with you. This would have come up no matter what you decided. This is about me, for me. Can't you see that?' My appetite gone, I threw my sandwich to Meg. She growled at Russell and ran down the hall with the food.

'I see a woman who's afraid to be alone.'

'This is the first man I've been willing to risk in sixteen years. If I'm afraid of anything I'm afraid I'll screw this up. I don't know how to do this anymore.' Actually, I'd never known how to do it. 'By some miracle a man I've liked for years has fallen in love with me. A nice, kind man loves me and I love him back. I want to make it work. Is that so awful? I'm sorry if that doesn't fit in with your view of feminism or social mores, or anthropological reasoning, but this is my life.' I sat back in my chair, confident that Chloe had been put firmly in her place. I calmly awaited the apology which I was due.

'Exactly. Listen to yourself. You just said it all. This is your life, not your parents', not mine, not my father's, and not Elliott's. This is your life and your time to make decisions for yourself. You don't have to think about anybody but yourself this time.'

'I am thinking about myself. I like having someone in love with me. I like the idea of having a baby. I don't even know if that's possible, but if it is I don't have much time to think about it. I need to make some decisions and I need to make them pretty damned fast.'

'The only decision you need to make is whether or not you are going to live your life. You have spent the first forty-three years of your life doing what you thought you had to do. When are you going to do something that is not determined by someone else?'

'Right now. I don't have to put up with this crap. How dare you? How dare you tell me how to live my life? You have been raised with such care, such privilege. What do you think your life would have been if I had put myself first the last sixteen years? What do you think our financial situation would be if our family hadn't given a thought to the generations coming up? It is terribly easy to talk about this sort of thing when you have already reaped the benefits. I put you first because that is what a parent does. I haven't been a martyr, I've been a responsible person. I have done the right thing and I have done it cheerfully. I'm not asking for sympathy or gratitude, but I will insist on respect.' Russell crawled under the kitchen table, eyeing me fearfully. I wondered if my voice sounded as shrill to his ears as it did to mine.

'I do respect and even admire you. I just feel like you have a chance to do anything you want for the first time in your life. You are smart and beautiful and you have a shit load of money. There is a big world out there. You don't have to spend the rest of your life in the kitchen or the nursery. The world needs smart, beautiful people.' She looked briefly around the kitchen. 'Just don't rush into anything and for God's sake make him wear a condom.'

'Do as I say, not as I do?'

'Pretty much.'

'Have you ever been to Wales?' Elliott was hanging up his jacket in my bedroom closet.

'I don't think I ever got that far, why?' I sat on the sofa and sipped at the champagne he'd brought to celebrate our first night together. I was relieved it was a bottle and not a black garter belt with a nippleless bra. I knew some men loved that sort of thing, but I knew it wouldn't be my best look. I was more the tartan knee-length nightshirt type.

'I've gotten to the point with the book where I need to spend a month or two in Cardiff this summer.' Elliott was writing one of those huge tomes academics are always working on. This one dealt with the tin mines of Wales and their influence on life as we know it, or something like that. 'I thought you might come along. We can arrange to go while Ben is at camp.'

'Let me think about it. I have Dad's things to settle and

I'm going to California at the end of May for Chloe's graduation.'

He sat on the arm of my sofa and kissed the top of my head. His hand wandered down and lightly brushed my breast. 'It wouldn't be all work. We could rent a house on the water, have a working honeymoon.' He slid down next to me and began to kiss my neck. 'Tea at four, fucking at five. We could save the cream tarts from tea and eat them off each other's bodies.' His hand wandered to a more central location, alerting my senses and clouding my judgment.

'A honeymoon?' I stopped fumbling with his belt buckle and looked at him.

He took my face in his hands and held it close to his. 'Marry me, Jill. Will you marry me in June?'

'Yes.' It seemed like the only reasonable answer.

'Do we tell Chloe this morning?' Elliott pulled a robe on over his freshly showered body. I remained in bed, marveling that I had another morning person in my life. I'd have to train him never to ask significant questions before nine.

'Not yet.' I pulled the duvet under my chin releasing a smell vaguely reminiscent of newly baked bread. Maybe that's what Chloe meant about baking bread for Elliott. She of all people would know what a well-laid bed smelled like. 'As she reminded me yesterday, this is my life, not hers.'

Elliott sat on the bed and threw the duvet off my legs. He kissed my knee and circled my ankle with his large hand. 'Don't you think she'll approve?'

'I know she won't.' His hand wandered up my leg. 'She thinks I need to take some time before I make any plans with you.' I should have been sated from the night before, but my body wiggled eagerly as his hand climbed.

He licked my kneecap and I noticed that his robe hadn't been tied properly. 'I plan to make you very happy.' And that morning he did.

'Mother, this is Mrs Bencivenga, Will's mother.' Chloe closed the living-room doors with a bang, enclosing the three of us in the room.

I held my hand out to her tentatively. 'I'm Jill Parkhurst.' Chloe had only told me that she wanted me to meet someone.

'I know I should have called but I was afraid you wouldn't see me.' A small, dark woman with tightly permed hair, she still held a black, soft-sided carry-all in her left hand.

'When did you arrive?' Had she been standing in the hall while Elliott's robe was flapping open?

'This morning. I came directly from the airport.' She shrugged her shoulders and stared at the floor.

'You must be tired. I'll get some coffee, or would you prefer tea?'

'Thank you. Coffee would be nice.' She smiled at me, her mouth crowded with small, sharp teeth.

'It will only be a few minutes. Why don't you make yourself comfortable while Chloe and I see to coffee. There is a powder room under the stairs if you would like to freshen up.' From the looks of her, she would need a day at Elizabeth Arden's to 'freshen up'. She wore tight denim jeans topped with a skinny knit top. She had thrown a faded ski jacket over her shoulders, ski passes still attached. Her almost childish body suggested a marathon runner or an aged gymnast.

'Could I use the phone? I want my husband to know I got here all right. This is the first time I've flown and I've been kind of nervous.' She bobbed her head at me. 'I brought a phone card.' She announced this last as though telephone credit cards were an item of great rarity.

'Of course. There is a telephone on the desk in the corner.' I heard my voice cramping into the distinctive 'Long Island lockjaw' I fell into at moments of great annoyance. 'Will you help me, Chloe?'

'I don't think this is such a big deal. We give her a cup of coffee and stick her in a cab back to the airport.' Chloe slammed three coffee mugs of dubious vintage on a plastic tray. Clearly she was choosing the ugliest items the kitchen had to offer. 'She certainly wasn't invited.'

'The woman has come all the way from wherever and I don't think we should show her the door until she has had her say.' I carefully measured coffee beans into the electric grinder. Unlike my daughter, I wanted to impress the woman with how well we did things. I wanted her to know what a careful family we were. I wanted things to be beautiful and correct. 'Put out proper cups on a decent tray, Chloe. The quickest way to get rid of her is to be cool and controlled. Formal attitudes, formal service.'

'She can drink out of the damn coffee pot for all I care. What nerve to show up out of the blue.' She arranged Coalport cups on a mahogany tray. 'Bet you anything she doesn't have a hotel room. Probably figures she can stay here.' Chloe slammed the old mugs back into a cupboard and stuffed the plastic tray behind a cabinet.

'She won't stay here long, I assure you. We give her a cup or two of coffee and a chance to say what she wants to say. You have made your decision and she will have to accept that.' I poured hot water into the cafetière and set the timer for three minutes.

'I don't see why I should have to listen to her at all. She is nothing to me. Her son is nothing to me.'

'Her son got you pregnant. She feels, I suppose, that she has some vested interest. I can understand that, I can sympathize with her. I felt the same way.' I put small damask napkins on the tray. 'She shouldn't be here, but she is. We listen and we send her on her way.'

'I hope it'll be that easy. This woman is a pro. She's one of those people who hangs around abortion clinics waving rosaries. Will called her a "sidewalk counselor".'

'Oh gag.'

'Exactly. I'm afraid she'll be here all day and all night. If we kick her out she'll probably pull out a bullhorn and start singing "Jesus Loves the Little Children" in the streets.'

'There isn't much she can do, dear. This is our home and we have every right to make her leave when we choose. I also will not hesitate to call the police if she creates any problems inside or outside the house.' I had attended grammar school with the chief of police, and the county sheriff's wife had wept at my father's funeral. If need be, I would work those facts into the conversation with the frizzy-haired little woman.

'I hope you're right.'

The timer went off and I plunged the filter down. 'Grab the tray, kiddo. This shouldn't take long.'

'Mrs Bencivenga . . .' I couldn't imagine a person I wanted less in my home.

'Please call me Maggie. It's short for Magdalena.' She stepped toward me as though the use of her nickname cemented an intimacy.

I took a step backwards. 'Please sit down.' I indicated a sofa near the large bank of windows.

'This is a wonderful house.' She smiled up from the sofa in such a manner that I suspected she'd done this before. Perhaps she had canvassed for Ronald Reagan or sold cosmetics door-to-door.

'Thank you.' I sat down in a chair near the now cold fireplace. 'Chloe, come sit down, please.' I waited for Chloe to sidle over to a chair. She watched the woman as though she expected her to strike out. I winked at her, reassuring her of a mother lion on her side.

'Have you come all the way from Colorado?' I strung out the syllables in the state's name. I tried to make it sound as foreign as possible. I wanted her to feel as foreign as possible.

'Utah. Park City, Utah.'

'I see. You have come a very long way so we will offer hospitality for a very brief time. I don't want to appear ungracious, but my father died on Thursday and we are a house in mourning.' I sat on the edge of my chair, stiff-backed. I wanted her to have no doubt as to the audacity of her actions. 'Cream and sugar?' I poured her coffee.

'I am so sorry. I had no idea about your father. Will didn't tell me anything.'

'Will called in the middle of the reception. He knew about my grandfather.' Taking her cue from me, Chloe's posture mirrored my own.

'I think he must have been so upset about the baby that he just forgot to mention it.' She pointed at the coffee tray. 'Cream please.'

I poured a small amount of skim milk into her cup. 'I'm afraid that your first plane trip is a complete waste of time. Chloe has made her plans.' I glanced at my watch. 'My schedule is rather full this afternoon, but feel free to enjoy your coffee. Even today, I can spare ten minutes.'

'I want you both to know how sorry our whole family is that this happened. We never had any trouble with Will before this. He's really a wonderful boy and I hope you won't think unkindly of him.' She directed this last comment to me.

'Why would I think ill of someone who impregnates my teenage daughter and then sends his mother to sort things out?' I took a sip of the coffee.

'Mrs Parkhurst, I wish it hadn't happened, but there is a

reason for everything. My children were all adopted. All three of them were conceived out of wedlock. I thank God every day for the love those women showed in having those babies and giving them to me. Those "mistakes" have given me and my husband the family we never thought we could have. Whenever I hear about a situation like your daughter's I want to tell my story.' She leaned forward eagerly, the coffee cup rattling against the saucer.

'You have told your story. I'm sure that Chloe payed close attention and will think about what you've shared.' I put my cup back on the tray, hoping she would see that I, at least, was done with this interlude in my busy day.

'But I haven't told you my story. I want to tell you why I couldn't have children. You need, you both need to hear this.' A tiny bubble of spittle formed at the corner of her mouth.

'Mrs Bencivenga, I'm sure that whatever . . .' I was wondering how I could backpedal on my offer of ten minutes. I'd never considered what a terribly long time ten minutes can be. Already I was beginning to shift in my seat and had recrossed my ankles twice.

'Go ahead.' Chloe leaned into the back of her chair and rested her elbows on the high arms. She appeared to be completely relaxed except for the play of muscles in her jaw.

'I grew up in a little town in Arizona. Burleys wasn't much to look at and had even less going on. We had about two thousand people, a few stores, and a gas station. My family lived a couple of miles outside of town on a farm. When I was sixteen I got pregnant. It wouldn't have been much of a problem, lots of girls were two or three months gone by the time they got married.' She licked her lips and took a sip of her coffee. 'But I had big plans. I was going to get out of Burleys and nothing was going to stop me. The boy, the father, was Burleys through and through.

He was never going to leave and I knew it. I knew if I had that baby I would never get out.

'My mother's younger sister lived up in Winslow. She was a waitress, at least most of the time. I wrote to her because she was the only person I knew who might know how I could get rid of it. She was kind of the black sheep. She was the one nobody liked to talk about much.'

She cleared her throat and looked at Chloe. 'I want you to know how it was for me. I couldn't tell my folks, for lots of reasons. I didn't have any money and I was so scared. I was still in high school and throwing up in the girls' lavatory. I was so scared. I didn't think I had any choices, not good ones anyway.'

'Go on.' Chloe's voice was pitched higher than usual, but her jaw muscles had relaxed.

'I used to babysit, so I'd saved enough for a bus ticket to Winslow. My aunt said she'd loan me the money for the rest, for the abortion. She took me to an ugly little house. I still remember the address, 49 Elm Street. In the back of the house was a little workshop kind of a place. I remember it had a sign hanging over the door, "the dog house". I guess it was a joke, like he was always in the dog house. My aunt took me back there and handed me over to this man and gave him an envelope. He told her he would drop me at her place after he was done.

'He seemed like a nice man and the room looked clean. After my aunt left he looked in the envelope and counted out the money. He said it was twenty dollars short and asked me to pay up before he did the business. I didn't have any more money and told him I would send it to him after I got home. He said he didn't do anything on credit, but maybe we could work something out.' She pushed the frizzy curls away from her face. 'Some might call it prostitution, but I know it was rape. I had to let him rape me before he would kill my baby.'

CHAPTER ELEVEN

The room was quiet and I fought the urge to speak, to comfort the woman. Clearly I wasn't the intended audience, so I looked at Chloe, whose face remained impassive.

'He had me and he knew it. I couldn't tell anybody what happened. I'd had an abortion and I'd committed an act of prostitution. He didn't take me back to my aunt's house. He said he didn't want anybody to see us together so he made me leave through the alley. He told me I'd have cramping and lots of bleeding, but I shouldn't go see any doctor. I told him I knew that much. I didn't bleed much, but I was awfully sick. I was burning up and a nurse friend of my aunt's brought me some pills that helped. After a few days the baby came out.' Here she paused and dabbed at her eyes with her fingers. 'It was in two pieces.' She rose from her chair and stood looking out the window before she turned back to Chloe.

'I got out of Burleys, but I had to whore and kill to do it. I married a good man and found out that murderer had scraped me out so good, nothing would ever grow inside of me.' Now she turned to me. 'A day doesn't go by that I don't see the pieces of that baby. Is that what you want for your daughter? A hell she can't escape?' She rubbed at her eyes like a sleepy child. 'Give life a chance, Chloe. If you don't want this baby, lots of other people do. Adoption will let you walk away and start fresh.'

'No. You're wrong. You don't walk away after an adoption. It haunts you. Can you imagine having a child somewhere in the world and you know you will never see it again? Do you know what it's like to see a child the same age and wonder if your child is happy, if he's even alive? It is hell. To use your words, "a hell you can't escape".' I began to cough and feared I would vomit. My hands shook and my chest hurt.

'But to give a child life is a blessing, and to share that child with another family is a wonderful thing to do.' She now had the zealot's light in her eyes.

'I'll be right back.' I somehow stood and forced myself through the doors into the powder room where I watched the remains of my breakfast and lunch twirl down the porcelain bowl. The skinny little woman in the worn ski jacket had locked me into a game of dueling tragedies and I debated whether or not to up the ante. She had laid her past out as neatly as a game of solitaire, but I still kept mine face down on the table. I rinsed my mouth and adjusted the collar on my blouse. 'Bitch.' I opened the door and entered the hall.

Chloe had moved to the window seat under the bank of windows. She sipped at a crystal tumbler and nodded as the woman spoke.

The woman turned as I walked into the room. 'I was just telling Chloe about some of the services available to girls.' She smiled brightly with the good news of service to girls.

'Services?' I could imagine the wide range of services the Magdalena Bencivengas of the world could provide. She would say the rosary for her. Perhaps she could put her on a prayer list, after she has shown her pictures of dead fetuses. 'What sort of services?'

'Counseling and financial help if needed.' She glanced around the room and shrugged. Clearly she understood that Chloe didn't need financial 'services'.

'If Chloe decides counseling is in order, arrangements will be made.'

'I can give her the names and numbers of women and girls who are birth mothers. I can also have some girls call who had abortions and know now what they really did.' She smiled gently. 'The girls who placed their babies are much happier than those who killed their children. And I don't think we've talked about keeping the baby at all. I don't know about you Jill, but I'm just about ready for my first grandbaby.' She sat next to Chloe and patted her on the knee.

'How dare you?' My voice roared in my ears although I probably did little more than whisper. 'How dare you come into my home uninvited and subject us to your tawdry little drama?' I walked over and slapped her hand away from Chloe's knee. 'If you don't leave this minute I will have the police drag you away.' The air was hot in my lungs.

'God forgive you for being so blind.' She made the sign of the cross and looked down.

'And may She forgive you for being so stupid. May She forgive you for looking for easy solutions to horrible problems. May She forgive you for tearing babies out of their mothers' arms and not giving young girls a second chance. And may She forgive you for not forgiving yourself. You did what you had to do, you stupid little cow! You did the only thing you could do. It may be the only really brave thing you ever did, but you did it.' My legs trembled and I put my hands on a table to steady myself.

'I'm not leaving. I'm not leaving this house until I know this baby is safe. I prayed all the way here that Chloe would come to know God and the truth. My prayers will be answered and this child will be safe.'

Chloe laughed and pulled her hair off her flushed face. 'Too late, Magdalena. Is that your real name?' Her words were slightly slurred. 'I have a story too. I listened to you. Your turn, so listen up.' She burped and wiped her mouth. 'I just drank pennyroyal and vodka. Problem solved.' She climbed off the love seat and sank into the sofa. 'Give me a few hours and I'll be right as rain.'

'Pennyroyal and vodka?' The vodka certainly explained the slurring and burping. 'What's pennyroyal?'

'Herb, variety of mint. Ancient form of birth control and abortifacient.' She swung her head as the last word dragged out of her mouth. 'I've done my research.' She held one finger up as though making a profound point. 'Works seventy-five times out of a hundred. Do you know that women have always known what to do? No problems till men took over medicine.' She turned and looked at Will's mother. 'I just took myself over.'

I walked over to the door and picked up the carry-all that Maggie had left on the floor. I picked it up, surprised at how heavy it was. Opening the front door I placed it on the steps and returned to the living room. 'I'll call you a cab. Please wait outside.'

'Why this way, Chloe?' I watched her, looking for external signs of her solution, her leap into do-it-yourself gynecology.

'It was mentioned in a book I read last semester. All kinds of home-grown birth control that work, for one reason or another. Women in Russia still use half a lemon scooped out and filled with honey as a diaphragm. Works pretty well, I guess.' She yawned as the vodka shuttled through her veins.

'But why did you try this?' It had never occurred to me to even learn how to change a tire or cut my own hair.

'I liked the idea. People say it's between a woman and her doctor. Who the hell is the doctor that he has a say? I needed to do it this way. I told you I didn't want to get in those stirrups.' She shut her eyes and rolled on her side.

'I think we'd better get you to the doctor and make sure everything is all right.' I glanced at my watch. 'We'd better hurry. It's almost five.' The alternative would be dragging her into the emergency room with all the cut chins and chest pains.

'No way. The whole point was to leave the doctors out of this. I should start bleeding in a few hours. A normal period.' She opened her eyes and focused on me with bleary eyes. 'And a hangover.'

'That much is guaranteed.' Chloe was not much of a drinker, as far as I knew. 'Let's get you up to bed so you can sleep it off.' I helped her to her feet.

I'd dropped the rings into my hairpin box months ago when my father's care had required hands with short nails and no rings. They had been on my hands for most of my adult life. They had left their mark. The third finger on my left hand was still slimmer than its neighbors. Is it any wonder I hadn't dated with a combined weight of three and one half carats on my hand? I opened the small safe in my closet and removed the two velvet-lined drawers. I spread the contents across my bed and picked through the jewelry. A small pile grew, the rings, a string of graduated pearls, a gold bangle, and a pair of emerald earrings. I added to the pile some less valuable pieces, mostly silver things we'd bought on our honeymoon. I topped the mound with an amethyst pectoral cross that my father had been especially fond of.

I'd heard the cheerful snuffling of the dogs before Elliott knocked on my door. Without waiting for a reply he opened the door and put his head into the room. 'I used the key you gave me. I hope you don't mind.'

'Come in. I was just going through some things.' I'd given him the key yesterday in case I wasn't at home. I had assumed he would still use the doorbell if I were home. I'd also assumed he wouldn't feel free to walk into my room after a perfunctory knock on the door. I hoped he wasn't going to bring over his record collection and his cats.

'What are you doing?' He kissed the back of my neck leaving a damp spot. 'Rob a jewelry shop while I was out?'

'I'm taking these to Crawford's in the morning.' I indicated the pile with a jerk of my head while I carefully replaced the rest, mostly my mother's, in the trays. Crawford's was the store where the bulk of the pile had come from originally. I still went there two or three times a year to have things cleaned, repaired, sometimes restrung. I didn't know what the stuff was worth, but I knew Crawford's was fair and reliable.

'I'll drop it off for you. I have to go into town first thing in the morning anyway.' He removed his jacket and tossed it across my sofa.

'I have to do it, thanks anyway. I want them to sell these for me, but I may have to take some of it, the cross for instance, to an auction house.' You didn't see that many bishops with their noses pressed up to Crawford's window.

With the instincts of a historian, Elliott plowed to the bottom of the pile and pulled out my engagement and wedding rings. 'Don't you think you should save these for Chloe? I'd think she might want them someday.'

I leaned over and took the rings from him. 'Chloe will approve of what I'm doing.' I stuffed the rings and other pieces into a small pouch and weighed it in my hand. 'I'm sending the proceeds to the women's health center over in Leeds. I got a begging letter from them a few months ago which I ignored. I hope this will at least pay for a couple of months' rent.'

'Why not just send them a check? It seems silly to sell things like this.' Using the key, dumping his jacket, and giving financial advice. He reminded me of Russell on walks in the woods, lifting his leg and marking his territory.

'I want to give something, something that's tangible, away. You, of all people, should understand how I must feel about these rings. The pearls are the strand he gave me and I wore on our wedding day. The silver stuff was from our honeymoon and I certainly don't want that around.' I rummaged in the pouch for the cross. 'I'm selling this because I listened to his advice my whole life. I did what he wanted me to do and I wish I'd had the nerve and sense not to.'

'That's silly, Jill. Selling a cross doesn't change anything.' He sat next to me on the bed.

'It changes things for me, Elliott. I feel better knowing I've done it.' I pushed away his hand where it rested on my shoulder.

'Jill, I just think . . .'

'Elliott, I think I know what I'm doing. This is my home we are sitting in, and my jewelry we are discussing. Am I making myself clear?'

'Point taken. Let's start over. How was your day?' He lifted my hand and kissed the palm. A peace offering.

'You first, mine will take longer.'

'It was fine. What's going on?'

'This afternoon the mother of the kid who impregnated Chloe showed up out of the blue. She flew all the way from Utah to tell Chloe about an abortion she'd had when she was a kid.'

'Good grief. How awful.'

'Her name is Magdalena, Maggie for short. She cried, she prayed, she crawled on her belly like a reptile.'

'What did you do?'

'You can imagine, the usual. I gave her the cold shoulder and then lost my temper and called her a stupid cow. Not that she wasn't, but I didn't have to say it.' I could have been kinder, but it wouldn't have changed anything.

'And Chloe?'

'Chloe sat there sipping a concoction that this very minute is wending its way to her womb and ending her pregnancy.' I smiled at him. 'Pretty ballsey kid, isn't she?'

'What did she take? Have you taken her to the doctor?'

'She took vodka and pennyroyal. She did the research and decided this is how she wanted to do it.'

'I think you should call poison control and make sure that she's not in any danger.'

'No, absolutely not.' Now he was giving me advice on being a mother.

'Why? She might have taken a toxic dose.'

'Because she knows what she wants. I'm trusting her judgment, which is exactly what I would like you to do for me.' I stood up. 'I'm going to check on Chloe. Why don't you go down and see what we have for dinner?' I was willing to let him make some decisions for me.

Her face was serene, her breathing steady. It hadn't started yet, but I knew it would. Seventy-five out of a hundred isn't a sure thing, but somehow I knew this was. That little cluster of cells would slough off and she would have her life back. Susan said abortion wasn't an eraser, but this seemed pretty close to it. No white gown, no stirrups, no suction, and no probing fingers.

Certain traits can skip generations. Height, color, musical ability. I wondered if nerve was one of those traits. Nerve, for lack of a better term. Not as noble as courage, but infinitely more useful. Nerve allows you to do what is best for yourself, say what you mean, and get what you need. My mother was subtle, but she had it. My father had nerve in his holy way. Perhaps it almost spent on them and had to recoup in the DNA, expand again before it could be passed on to my daughter. If she got it from them it must have passed through me. Maybe a little of it still clung under the bone.

'I'm going to have a glass of wine. Do you want anything?' I looked for a bottle of Merlot while Elliott made a salad.

'I'll pass. I think you'd better not have any either. If we're going to try to conceive you should start treating your body as though you already have. We should pick up some pre-natal vitamins tomorrow and get you started on those.' He tossed a handful of red onions into the wooden bowl. 'I also think we should forget about contraception starting tonight. Considering your age, this could take a while.'

'As I was saying, I'm going to have a glass of wine.' I pulled the bottle from the rack.

'Jill, are you saying you don't want to have a child? I thought we were agreed on that.' He had a pained expression on his face and a tomato in his hand.

'On some levels I find the idea awfully appealing, but I think we should be realistic.'

'Now I'm not being realistic?'

'Elliott, I'm forty-three years old. I'm not exactly at the peak of my fertility and neither are you. You want me to take pre-natal vitamins and get all excited about some phantom baby that's swimming up and down in your brain. Let's go buy nursing bras and a crib while we're at it.' I pulled the corkscrew out too soon and left half the cork wedged in the bottle. 'Fuck it.'

'Give me that.' Elliott quickly extracted the cork and handed the bottle back to me. 'I thought we were in agreement Jill, I want to make a life. I want to create a family.'

'We've got families. We each have a child.'

'I always wanted to have more children. Sally was busy with her dissertation and we kept putting it off. This is my last chance, darling. Can't you see that?'

'Elliott, if a baby is that important to you, maybe you shouldn't be in my bed. If you want babies, you should avoid women with gray hair and laugh lines.'

'Age isn't that much of an issue anymore. Some wonderful things are being done with hormone treatments these days. We can at least try.'

'Do you have any idea of what you are proposing? Pump me full of hormones, make love according to the clock and the calendar, for what?'

'For a child, our child! A child that will give us both a fresh start.'

'A fresh start? That's a hell of a lot to ask of a baby. Elliott, I've spent the last eighteen years taking care of a child and I'm not sure if I want to start this all over again. I'm not saying it is totally out of the question, I just wish you would stop regarding it as a done deal.'

'Look, I've told you how important this is to me. If you can't get pregnant I can live with that. I just want you to try, agreed?'

'Let me get this straight; if I really love you I will try to conceive a child that I may or may not want? I don't think so.'

'So where does that leave us?' He chopped at the tomato until it resembled a little battlefield.

'Wherever we want to be. What kind of dressing do you want on that?'

'Forget the damned dressing! Forget the food. I need to know what's really going on. I love you, but you keep running hot and cold. We talk, but I don't think we hear each other. We have great sex, but I don't feel like I've really been intimate with you. I never really get into you.' He tossed the knife into the sink. To keep from using it on me?

'Not much like it was with Sally, is it?' Not a challenge; more a diagnosis of a terminal illness. I knew dying when I saw it.

'This isn't about Sally and you know it. It's about us and what we can have together.'

'It's about expectations, and I'm afraid that I will never live up to yours.' I realized, with relief, that I no longer had to.

CHAPTER TWELVE

'I'll call you in the morning. We both need a good night's sleep.' Elliott kissed my forehead and held me against his chest for a moment. If he wanted to pretend exhaustion I wouldn't object.

'In the morning then.' I tucked a bit of hair behind his ear and smiled at him.

'It's going to be fine, darling. Besides, we don't have to dread our first fight any longer at least.' He pulled out his car keys.

'Yes, I suppose there's that.'

'Goodnight, darling.' He kissed me quickly and walked toward his car.

'Goodnight.'

It was hardly noticeable. The size of a quarter. I was sure her sheets at school had bigger spots. Knowing how she hated to do laundry I'd never dared to ask how often she laundered her sheets.

I stripped the bed quickly, and spread out replacement sheets that smelled of lavender and cedar. I rolled the used sheets carefully so the spot was in the middle. Certainly it was only the normal flow, a part of the normal cleansing. I wouldn't think about the other part, the part that wasn't going to happen. I would rinse the spot out in the laundry room with cold water. Wash it down.

I turned down the corner of the bed and fluffed the pillows. Still a girl's room, it was snug and inviting. A perfect place for a girl with cramps. I'd make her tea and toast so she wouldn't have to take aspirin on an empty stomach.

I knocked on her bathroom door. 'Chloe, I'll be back in a few minutes. I want to run your sheets down to the laundry room and get us some tea.'

'Thanks, Mom. I got some blood on my nightshirt and panties if you want to take those too. The door's unlocked.' She shouted over the noise of the shower.

I opened the door and shoved the small pile of clothes on top of the sheets. I could see her outline through the steamy shower door. She hummed a tune I didn't recognize as she rubbed a washcloth between her legs.

I hurried out the door through the darkened house. Twelve o'clock and all was well. Her plan had worked and ended in a bit of extra laundry and a song in the shower.

I turned on the cold tap at the old soapstone sink. I picked up her panties and ran my finger lightly across the silky fabric, around the rich, wine-colored stain. What had she said; less than half an inch? Just a normal flow. A flow that carried away my first grandchild. I turned off the water.

I carefully folded the sheet, making certain the spot was folded to the top. I folded her Tweetie Bird nightshirt twice. The first time the bird's strange fetus-like head grinned at me. The second time I folded it carefully so that Tweetie was hidden on the bottom. I placed the panties on top and put the pile on the shelf above the washer to be dealt with in the morning.

'How are you feeling this morning?' Chloe wandered into the kitchen before seven.

'I feel great. I was a little crampy last night, but this morning I just feel great.' She pushed up the sleeve of her sweater as she reached for the coffee pot. 'Where's Elliott this morning?'

'He didn't stay last night. We were both tired and so he left.' I shrugged to show my lack of concern.

'Have you decided what you are going to do? About Elliott, I mean.'

'I don't think I have to do anything about him. He wants something I don't think I can give him, not any more. He wants what he calls a fresh start. New wife, new baby. I think he really needs some nice grad student.' Oddly enough I didn't seem to mind that morning.

'I do think he loves you, though.' She blew on her coffee.

'I love him too. I just don't love him enough to go back twenty years and live the rest of my life living out his little fantasy of the perfect life.'

'Do you have any fantasies of your own? What do you want to do?'

'I don't know. I think the smoke needs to settle before I can think clearly.' The place felt like a battlefield that morning. The day after, when things are quiet, but a little smoke still hangs in the air.

'I hope you don't go on being the Widow Parkhurst.'

'What do you mean?'

'Using all that brave young widow junk. The memory of my philandering father doesn't seem like much to hang your life on.' She spread marmalade on a slice of toast.

'Your grandmother told you?' I now understood why Eleanor wouldn't be attending Chloe's graduation.

'She was full of it. She was trying to defend her son, but it didn't quite work.'

'Oh Chloe, I'm so sorry. Your father was a wonderful young man. The fact that he made a mistake . . .'

'It's not important. I really don't care. I never knew the

man and whatever he did or didn't do has nothing to do with me.' She shoved her toast aside and leaned across the table toward me. 'He is a tiny part of my past. I don't care about any of that. I care about the future and I make those decisions. I decide about tomorrow.'

'I just want you to know that he did love you. You were loved and wanted by both of us.'

'I know that. I've never really doubted it for a minute.' She sipped at her coffee and set the mug down. 'You should also know that Grandma told me about the other baby. I don't want you dragging that around any longer.'

'What did she tell you?' I felt as though I was reading my obituary in the newspaper.

'As much as she knew. She said you'd been sent to England and the baby had been put up for adoption. She said it was a boy. Is that right?'

'That's right. A beautiful baby boy. I wanted to keep him, but I didn't see how I could.' I didn't see the need for details.

'Do you know where he is? Have you looked for him?'

'No.' A lie. I'd been looking in boys' faces for years. 'I don't know anything other than he was placed in Britain with a "good family". I won't look for him because I don't deserve him. I didn't fight for him.' The front of my face felt heavy with tears and I stared at my hands.

'I can guess how it must have been. I remember how formidable Grandmother could be. Combine that with Grandpa when he was doing his God Incarnate bit and you never stood a chance.'

'Yeah, that's what I've always told myself.' I looked at her. 'You wouldn't have been bullied. You weren't bullied. You did what was best for you and I am in such awe of that. I am in awe that a daughter of mine knows her own mind so well.'

'You've always known your own mind, you just haven't

known how to use it. You have always worked from the
back, pretending to say what you mean but skirting around
it. Seeming to do what you want, but never quite. You and
Grandma are so much alike.'

'Eleanor?' I was appalled.

'The one and only. The two of you wheedle, manipulate,
give presents, and get in people's faces. You both have so
much spirit, so much power, but neither one of you will
claim it. Instead you just kind of leak it out in bits of rage
and frustration. You both lose your tempers, drink too
much, eat too much, drive too fast.'

'Eleanor and I are the same?' I shuddered at the words.

'With one exception.'

'What is that?' Her nails were longer than mine?

'You are capable of change. There is hope for you.'

I found a weathered fruit box in the back of the garage that
would do. It measured about two by two and a half feet. It
was about a foot and a half deep and seemed to be of
sturdy construction. A piece of plywood at the back of the
garden shed could be cut down to serve as a lid. I grabbed
a rusted shovel and set out to the back of the grounds.

Susan and I had always buried things in the back. The
ground was soft there and it was nice to have all the baby
birds, half-eaten mice, stillborn puppies, and roadkills in
the same general area. Nothing had been buried there for
over thirty years, but the ground remained soft. In spite of
that it took me over an hour to dig a sufficient hole and my
arms and shoulders ached before I tossed the shovel aside.
I arched my back and heard minute cracking as I looked
with satisfaction at my handiwork. I pulled down some
small fir branches from a nearby tree and lined the hole so
it would smell nice. I carried the box into the mudroom off
the kitchen.

I'd thought about what I needed while I dug so it didn't

take long to gather it all together. The veil and silk stockings from my wedding day were in the back of my closet. My father's pectoral cross was still in the bag to be delivered to the jeweler. A copy of my son's adoption papers were in my father's files under 'Jill, St Marys'. Along with my mother's hat that I'd worn to my father's funeral, I grabbed the pink confection she'd worn to my wedding. I laid my wedding veil in the box as a sort of liner. I left the ends hanging over the edges. Next, I layered the stockings and the hats. I slipped the pectoral cross in my pocket and went upstairs to rifle through my father's drawers, and pulled out a clerical collar as a replacement. The cross was worth too much money to the women's health center, after all. I spread the adoption papers over the collar and went to the laundry room.

I carried the bundle to the box and carefully arranged it to fit the contours. I folded the edges of the veil over, forming a tidy package. I kissed the top of the veil and smiled as I adjusted the plywood piece over the top. I nailed the lid down using six nails, not bending any of them. I sawed two inches off one end of the lid to make it look a bit neater. It had looked too slapdash with that bit hanging over.

Since this was a private ceremony I waited until Chloe went into town to rent a video and pick up the dry cleaning. I cut several blooms from the floral arrangements that were still scattered around the house. One of the most interesting items left over from the floral tributes was an arrangement of birds of paradise. I cut two, thinking they would look quite amusing, perhaps challenging, in the Connecticut wood that my backyard had become. I put the flowers into a canvas bag and hurried out the mudroom door, my arms weighted with flowers and memories.

The skies had clouded over while I'd been gathering the odd collection sheltered in the old fruit box. As I walked toward the back, large drops began to fall and I shivered inside my thin cotton sweater.

At the hole I put the box down and pulled a felt-tip pen out of my pocket to mark the box. I had intended to write my name and the date, but that seemed too much like writing a check or signing a tax return. After a moment's deliberation, with rain sliding down my face, I wrote 'A GIRL'S LIFE'. I added a squiggly little drawing of a daisy which I had used to dot the 'i' within Jill when I was ten. I settled the box into the hole.

After satisfying myself that it was as level as I could make it, I arranged the flowers around the top of the box. I withheld only the extravagant birds of paradise. The old box looked like one of those kitschy pictures sold at craft fairs. Old weathered boards with bright, fresh blooms painted over them. I shoveled dirt over the flowers as quickly as I could. I was relieved when the box was gone and nothing showed but fresh black dirt. I got on my knees and placed the birds of paradise in an upright pose while I tapped the earth around them.

I closed my eyes and said a prayer, not to the god of my fathers, that Anglo-Catholic patriarch, but to someone older. I prayed to the one condemned men pray to when they call for their mothers. I prayed to the one who dresses in blue and hangs above a village in old Yugoslavia, pretending to be a virgin. I prayed to her because she would know what to do with a little soul who tried to come in to the world too soon. I prayed to that face we love first and best and prayed that the baby would be safe. I prayed that when the baby came to us again we would know who it was. It felt so good to talk to a woman instead of the one who, according to most reports, felt my sex was an afterthought, a necessary annoyance.

I threw the shovel into the underbrush and walked back to the house.

'Doing a little gardening?' Chloe, returned from her

errands, was making coffee in the kitchen when I came in. The dogs jumped on me with enthusiasm as they sniffed at my muddy clothes.

'No, I was putting something at the back of the property.' The coffee smelled wonderful and I was chilled to the bone.

'What couldn't wait until the rain cleared?'

'I was burying a box. I put some things in there that were a part of my life and I buried them.' It didn't sound as sensible now as it did an hour ago.

'What kind of things?' Chloe looked at me as though I had just started growing petunias out of my nose.

'Pour us some coffee and I'll tell you, after I get into some dry clothes.' I pulled my sodden sweater over my head as I headed into the hall.

I held my hands around the cup, grateful for the heat. 'First I want to clear something with you. Elliott thought you might object.'

'What's that?'

'I'm planning to sell some jewelry and give the money to the local women's health center. I'm planning to sell the things your father gave me and one of your grandfather's pectoral crosses. I know they need the money more than I need jewelry and frankly, I don't want to look at those things anymore. If you feel strongly, now is the time to let me know.'

'I think it's a great idea. Positively inspired.' She grinned over the rim of her coffee mug. 'Now, what was in the box?'

'I started to wash the stains out of your things last night, but I couldn't do it. I buried them along with my wedding veil, some hats, the adoption papers, and one of your grandfather's dog collars. I know it sounds silly, but I wanted a ceremony. I prayed to Mother Earth to watch over the baby and let us know when it comes back.' Tears gathered in my eyes and my voice caught. 'I couldn't just let it be washed away.'

'I think that's nice.' Chloe's face mirrored my own. 'I'm glad you did it, I really am.' She took a deep breath. 'This has been so awful. Last night I was so happy it was over, but I was so sad that the baby was gone.' She wiped her hand across her face. 'Thank you.'

'I marked the spot. I can show you where it is, if you want to see it.'

She nodded her head. 'Maybe later.'

I smiled at my daughter and tried to feel it inside. 'I don't know about you, but I've got a few other things to do today.'

'Oh, I almost forgot to tell you. Aunt Susan called while you were out. She wants you to call her later.'

'I think I'll just stop by. I feel like I need to get out of this house and do a little running around today.'

'You're going to hate me, I know you are.' Susan handed me a mug of tea and turned away from me.

'Susan, stop being silly.' Her face looked pinched and finally as old as my own. 'You can't have done anything I'd hate you for.'

'I shouldn't be talking about this to you or anyone else.'

'Then don't. You just keep quiet and I'll tell you about what's been going on since I saw you last.' It was, after all, the reason I'd driven to her house in the worst rain of the season.

'I slept with him.' She closed her eyes and made a wiping motion in the air. 'We didn't actually sleep, but you know what I mean.'

'Well, it's about time. Just last week you thought Fletch was never going to play "hide the sausage" again.' I lifted my mug at a jaunty angle. 'Congratulations.'

'Not Fletch, Michael. I slept with Michael.'

'You slept with the beautiful priest?' Susan was an extravagant flirt, but adultery was as foreign to her nature as chewing tobacco or nipple piercing. 'Whatever possessed you? When did this happen?'

'It was this morning.' She pulled the edges of her cardigan around her as though she was covering the place where the 'A' would be embroidered.

'This morning? Your kids are on break, Susan. Where were the kids? What the hell were you thinking?' I heard my voice rising.

'Kent took the kids into the city to see a movie.'

'What if they'd come home? What if your husband came home? Did you think of that?'

'Will you just shut up? Will you just shut up and listen to me? I've listened to you for months and months and now I need you to listen to me. Do you think you can do that?' Susan spat the words at me and then sat down heavily on the worn sofa in her sunroom.

I sat down next to her and took her hand in mine. 'You caught me by surprise. This is the last thing I expected to hear from you.'

'Pretty out of character, isn't it?' She smiled ruefully and squeezed my hand.

'I think you could say that.' It was akin to finding whips, chains, and a black leather mask among my father's effects.

'He stopped by to thank me for Easter lunch and before I knew it I was wrapped around him like stripes on a candy cane.'

'Why? He's absolutely darling, but this isn't like you.'

'I really don't know. Maybe it was that old thing; if you could do it and know you wouldn't get caught?'

'But you could have gotten caught.'

'Fletch got caught.'

'What do you mean?'

'I caught Fletch. He's sleeping with his secretary.'

'He told you that?'

'He didn't have to. I know all the signs. I should after all these years.'

'You mean he's done this before?' She'd never mentioned a word about it.

'Three or four times. Three times I know about and the fourth I suspect.'

'You never said anything. Why didn't you tell me?'

'I guess it wasn't quite real if I didn't talk about it. I would ignore it and it would go away.' She leaned her head against my shoulder. 'This time it's breaking my heart. I think he really loves her. It's not just sex this time.'

'I don't understand any of this. At Easter he was saying he wanted another baby. You don't want babies if you're in love with another woman.'

'He loves me the way I was, Jill. He loves the me that stayed home and who was always pregnant or nursing. He loves the me that was car-pooling Kent to soccer and Lucy to ballet classes.'

'That's who he knows.' It's certainly who I knew.

'I realize that. That's who I've been, but I can't stay that way forever. I need to think about what's next for me, for us. I need him to really look at me, not just the mother of his brood.'

'Is that why you were with Michael? Were you trying to get Fletch's attention?'

She laughed softly and shook her head. 'I haven't been with another man for over twenty years. I wanted to make sure I could be with someone else before I decided to leave Fletch.'

'You're going to leave Fletch for Michael?' I wondered if she realized how little a priest earned.

'Of course not, Jill. If I leave Fletch it's certainly not going to be because of Michael. I just wanted to have sex with someone who had as much reason as me to keep his mouth shut.'

'So, how was he?' God knows I'd wondered enough myself.

'Just like Fletch; a one-minute missionary man.'

'What a disappointment.'

'Tell me about it. First time I commit adultery and I don't even break a sweat.'

'Maybe it doesn't count if you don't break a sweat.' I looked at her and raised my eyebrows.

'We'll have to ask a priest and find out.'

CHAPTER THIRTEEN

I closed the study doors and looked at him for a moment before I spoke. 'Whatever were you thinking of?'

'I'm sorry?' He looked at me with confusion. I told him I'd wanted to give him something of my father's as a thank you for his help.

'I've spoken to Susan.'

'I see.' Michael turned away from me. 'What did she tell you?' He blushed bright red, probably more embarrassed by his poor performance than the moral quagmire he'd shoved his genitals into.

'She told me she'd just found out her husband was in love with another woman. Did she tell you that?'

'No, she just said – never mind.'

'She said she wanted you so your "boon companion" decided to rise to the occasion?' I sat down and motioned for him to do the same. 'Don't they tell you how to handle these things in seminary? Isn't there some kind of course on how to keep your trousers zipped?'

'Admittedly I was wrong, but I don't think it's your place to set me straight. This is between myself—'

'You are a priest who has just nailed my best friend, who

you met in my home. After you've had the unmitigated gall to sit in my home and lecture me about the morality of abortion and my lack of piety, I'll say whatever I please.' I paused for air before continuing. 'I have every right to lecture, harangue, and otherwise verbally abuse you, Father Michael.'

'I think I'm in love with her.' His words were slow and measured, treasures not to be wasted.

'You think you love her. You think you love her?' I grabbed a pillow from the sofa and threw it toward him. 'Of course you think you love her, you fool. Every man thinks he loves her. Every man thinks he loves every woman and that's how he excuses his overwhelming urge to stick his "boy wonder" into any warm damp orifice he comes across. Jesus fucking Christ.'

'You don't understand, Jill. It wasn't like that at all.'

'Michael, I don't want to hear what it was like. I don't want to hear that her soul spoke to yours or any of that crap. I want you to understand how powerful you can be and the damage you can cause as a man and as a priest. If you're going to fall back on "love" every time some poor woman shakes her skirts at you you'll be too busy taking your pants off to put your collar on. You'll destroy their lives, not to mention your own career.' I turned my head as I heard a noise behind me.

'You'll have to forgive Jill.' Elliott stood at the opened door and smiled at us. 'She prides herself on being unromantic.'

'How long have you been standing there?' I hadn't expected to see him again, at least not right away.

'Just enough to hear your speech about men and orifices. Don't worry, Michael, she doesn't stay angry.' He walked over and kissed the top of my head.

'I think I'd better be leaving now.' Michael rose without looking at me.

'Not yet, Michael. I told you I had something I wanted you to have.' I took a book from the table in front of us. 'This is a signed, first edition by Bishop Stansmere. Father didn't agree with him, for the most part, but he found him to be terribly interesting to read. As you no doubt know he was a member of the Sexual Freedom League back in the sixties. Of course that was also why he was defrocked, but I thought you two might have something in common.' I handed the book to him and he took it between two fingers.

'Thank you, Jill. I'll look forward to reading it. I'll see myself out.' He nodded to us and hurried out the door.

'What was that all about?' Elliott flopped into the seat Michael had vacated.

'I wanted to give him a book so I asked him to stop by.'

'What was all that I came in on?'

'We were just talking, Elliott.' I looked away from him and studied my fingernails. They were clean and neat, the way I thought my life should be.

'Obviously it was more than that, darling. You looked like you were ready to bite his head off.'

'Elliott, I really don't want to discuss this.'

'And I don't want us to have any secrets between us. That's not how I want us to be, how I want us to live.'

'I keep thinking about our conversation last night and I don't think there can be an "us".' Even though I said the words, the sound of them surprised me. I sounded as though I was returning a dress to a department store. 'I realized when I got this home that it wasn't quite what I was looking for. Can you please credit my account?'

'I thought you loved me. You told me you loved me.' Elliott's face had grown long and pale.

'I hope you understand, Elliott. I do love you, I just don't think I love you enough to share my life with you. You want things I'm just not interested in, not any longer.'

'What are you talking about?'

'I've lived my life by other people's rules. I need to find out what I want to do and what I can do. I've got to be on my own to do that.' I imagined my womb relaxing, no longer preparing for a guest.

'That is the most selfish, sophomoric thing I've ever heard an adult say.'

'Yes, I suppose it is.' Probably should have said it years ago.

Mary presented me with two fat folders. 'This is everything I could find, Jill. I went through these files about a year ago so everything should be fairly current.'

'Great.' I took the files from her eagerly and began to quickly thumb through the papers. 'Here it is.'

'Find what you were looking for?' She sat behind her desk, peering at me over her glasses.

'Yes ma'am. Thanks for your help, Mary. I'll give this back when I'm done.' I tucked the papers under my arm.

'Just toss them. It will save me the effort later.'

'Thank you for seeing me so quickly Mr Salter.' John Salter headed the Anglican World Services. His office in Manhattan was small and poorly finished as befitted an organization dedicated to the relief of suffering in developing countries. His secretary had given me an appointment as soon as she heard my father's name. I suspected she was looking forward to a gift of memorial funds.

'It's lovely to meet you. I was very fond of your father, all of us were. He was always a great supporter of our work.' About thirty, his appearance was surprisingly dapper for someone who shuttled powdered milk and rice to the starving. His wide-striped shirt and well-cut blazer were in sharp contrast to the picture above his desk of an African nurse cradling an emaciated child.

'Thank you. My father always spoke very highly of your work.' My father spoke very highly of almost everyone's work that fell under the Church's umbrella. He was a company man.

He smiled at me. 'My secretary said you were anxious to see me.' He nodded as though he could pump words out of me.

'Yes, I was, I am.' I pulled an envelope out of my purse and pushed it across his desk. 'There is a stipulation in my father's will that ten thousand dollars be given to a charity of my choosing. He wasn't able to keep up with current events those last few months and he wanted to make sure that these funds went to a relief organization which would put the money to the best immediate use.' A total fabrication. My father had decided months ago where every penny of his estate would go. The money was mine.

'This is wonderful, most generous.' He smiled at me while he opened the envelope. 'This is your résumé.' His smile faded.

'That's right. The money will go wherever I decide to go. I have never had a paid position, but if you'll look at my résumé you'll see that I have extensive fund-raising experience.' True, I'd kept the Derrytown Junior League in the black for years. Photographs of me, accepting large checks, had been a feature of the local paper for years. I could raise fifteen thousand without breaking a sweat. I could write two grants before lunch. I was certainly in the top ten of Connecticut's beggars.

'Mrs Parkhurst, I'm afraid we have a very small staff here at headquarters.' He stared at my purse, knowing he was saying goodbye to the money.

'I don't want to be in Manhattan. I want to be here, the

San Lucas Hospital in Baja.' I handed him the information I'd taken from my father's files.

'San Lucas has a handful of nurses, a couple of janitors. We keep one full-time doctor there and everyone else comes in from elsewhere on a voluntary basis.' San Lucas specialized in cranio-facial and orthopedic surgery.

'That's what I want to do. I want to volunteer. I don't need to be paid.'

'The volunteers are trained professionals. We need doctors and nurses. We need technicians and equipment.'

'You need money. I can raise funds for San Lucas. I'm very well connected and I'm not afraid to beg.' For money or a job.

'All fund-raising takes place here. If you want to come in here and volunteer a few hours a week, we can arrange something.'

I ignored his offer to stuff envelopes and answer the phones. 'In this letter my father received a few months ago, it said San Lucas needed one and a half million dollars to refurbish the operating theaters. How much has been raised so far?'

'Not much, I'm afraid. San Lucas is a fairly low priority right now. The last two years we've had to focus so much on famine relief that we're stretched pretty thin. As long as the hospital can keep the doors open we have to be satisfied with that, at least for now.'

'Give me six months. I will pay to get myself down there and make a contribution, in addition to the ten thousand, which will cover my room and board. If I haven't raised five hundred thousand by the end of that six months you can send me packing.' I was compiling a list of likely contributors as I spoke.

'Obviously any contributions will come from up here. Maybe you would be more effective if you stayed here to raise the funds.'

'No. I'll be more effective if I get my hands dirty.'

'Well, I guarantee you'll get your hands dirty in San Lucas.'

'Then we have a deal?' I placed the check on his desk.

He picked it up and looked at me. 'Don't drink the water and don't eat any unpeeled fruit.'

EPILOGUE

I didn't realize until tonight that my father died a year ago today. I was busy most of the day haggling over the price of a new generator. I'm not sure how we're going to pay for it, but I've got two foundations I haven't hit up for a few months.

In spite of John Salter's warnings about fruit and water, Montezuma and his infamous revenge managed to track me down. Combining Montezuma with heat, hard work, and the complete absence of any food I like to eat, the end of my first two months at San Lucas found me thirty pounds lighter. I hadn't been this thin since I was twenty so my clothes hung like socks on a rooster. Like most of the staff, I took to wearing surgical scrubs every waking moment. The combination of cool loose cotton and the fact that someone else launders them is irresistible to us. I wear mine with gaudy papier mâché jewelry from the markets so that I'm not confused with the medical staff. After two bouts with head lice I cut my hair to about an inch all over. I look like an aging Peter Pan in my green scrubs and silver fringe.

A few months ago I was offered the position of administrator, but I turned it down. Being in charge of fund-raising leaves me time to help in the hospital when things get hectic, which they usually do. I especially like the children's ward and they love my jewelry. Their favorite is a pink iguana. The iguana's tail is made of fat beads that seem to wiggle of their own volition. It's a real crowd pleaser.

Elliott is engaged now. I don't know her, but Susan said she is lovely. She's Elliott's age and has two grandchildren so I suppose he's finally gotten over his baby dreams. I sent him a note of congratulation, but haven't gotten a reply.

Susan had her tubes tied and enrolled in a Master's in Social Work program at Columbia. Fletcher moved in with his secretary, and came back with his tail tucked between his legs after six weeks. Susan took him back but he has to pick up the youngest child after school three days a week. Susan writes that they've never been closer. Go figure.

Bishop Mark died suddenly of a heart attack and was replaced with a nice liberal Yalie. Father Michael has been assigned to his staff and will no doubt climb quickly up the ecclesiastical ladder. In November he married a thirty-three-year-old restaurateur. This was her third marriage.

I met Chloe down in Cabo for Christmas. She's fine, but is just about ready to return to the bookstores and sushi bars in Berkeley. We went to a karaoke bar and performed a stunning rendition of White Christmas. The bar was selling margaritas half price so we managed to get some applause.

Chloe said she didn't care, so in January I put the house up for sale. I had my attorney arrange to have everything put in storage, so someday I suppose I'll have to go back and figure out what to do with the leavings.

I've been living in staff quarters for the last year, and for the most part that's worked out fine. I do have my eye on a little place about a mile from San Lucas. It was built by an American couple who thought they would retire here. Apparently they packed up after their first summer. If I can get it for the right price, I'll buy it. Something about it just feels right.